Summer
COWBOY

Cowboy Hero, Book 7

BARBARA MCMAHON

One

Becca Montgomery pulled the pick up truck into the almost empty graveled parking lot, dodging the large puddles, splashing through the smaller ones. The sun blazed in the freshly washed Wyoming sky. Dazzling reflections from the puddles almost blinded her. Nosing close to the weathered barn, she cut the engine. She slapped a Stetson on her head and opened her door to the windy morning.

It had stopped raining only a half hour before. The sun had quickly melted the lingering clouds. The wind blew the scent of damp grass across her cheeks. It was cool for late May. Invigorating. Once the series of storms passed, the temperature was bound to go up.

The low line of dark clouds on the western horizon threatened more rain. But for the moment, she'd enjoy the sunshine.

"I've had enough rain to last this year and next," she mumbled, walking quickly into the cavernous feed and grain store that catered to the ranchers for miles around.

It had rained for three solid days. Everything remained soggy from the wet spring. The last few days of rain had only worsened the situation. She had cattle knee deep in mud, fence posts washing away, soggy hay and mud slicks where feeder roads crisscrossed the range.

Instead of having the livestock trucks load cattle directly from staging areas out on the range, she'd now have to drive the cattle earmarked for the spring sale closer to a major road. A paved road.

Once the rain stopped and things could dry out a bit, that is. She so did not want to be out in a sloppy field trying to get recalcitrant cattle into a chute leading to a truck.

She stepped inside the huge double doors and tipped back her hat. Taking a deep breath, she smiled as the smells of Bob Mason's Feed and Grain filled her nostrils. Hay and leather, wood and oats; the scents mingled clean and fragrant. The huge old barn that housed the various accouterments needed by ranchers wasn't warm, the coolness from outside hit no barriers when the wind swirled through the open building.

Becca didn't notice. She was used to the place. She remembered visiting the store with her father when she'd been a little girl. The place had held magic back then. Now it seemed merely functional, but the scents still teased her imagination, sparked fond memories.

Walking to the back, to the long counter on which Bob Mason rested his elbows, she smiled in greeting. She'd known him all her life and continued doing business with him when her father died and left her the ranch. Bob was talking to a stranger, a tall man wearing the standard dark cowboy hat, jeans and boots.

Becca moved toward the other end of the counter, fiddling with some of the display items, content to wait until Bob was free.

"Need any help?" Bob called.

"I can wait," Becca replied, flashing a curious glance at the stranger.

"I'm surprised to see you. It's supposed to start raining again before long, which'll make it a mess driving," Bob commented genially. "If you need something, you could have called."

"A little rain never hurt anyone. Though if it doesn't let up soon, I may have a few drowned calves."

She looked straight at Bob, but could still see the stranger from the corner of her eye. He stood over six feet. His hat covered most of his hair, except for the dark strands that curled near his collar. His cheekbones were high and tautly covered, his jaw strong, stubborn. The broad shoulders of his denim jacket were damp, evidence he'd been in the rain before it stopped.

She turned back to the counter without looking her fill. She dare not give the stranger the wrong impression, though she angled herself so she could continue to watch him from the corner of her eye. One glimpse wasn't enough.

Something about him stirred her senses. She wished she'd checked her hair before she slapped her hat on.

She wondered who he was. Not from around here, that was for sure. She knew most of the cowboys in the area by sight if nothing more. Not that it made any difference. Once she ordered what she needed, she'd head for the post office to pick up the mail, then the lawyer's office.

Her immediate future didn't lie in Wyoming. She almost danced a quick two-step in anticipation.

A warm glow spread through her at the thought of her surprise. She'd waited a long time for this and her excitement grew as she drew closer to finally putting her plan in motion.

Only a few more days—

"Becca Montgomery," Bob interrupted her musing. From the way both he and the stranger looked at her she knew it wasn't the first time he'd called her.

"Yes?"

She turned to face Bob, her eyes drifting involuntarily to the stranger once again. His gaze met hers, held. For a split second her breath caught in her throat. Her heart pumped just a tad faster. He wasn't the best looking man she'd ever seen, but he came close. Who was he?

"I want you to meet a friend of mine from a long way back. Josh Randall. He's looking for a summer job. Thought you could use the help out at the Lazy M. I heard you lost a hand a few months back," Bob said.

Becca stepped closer, offering her hand to the tall cowboy. When he took it, a startling warmth flashed through her. Her breath caught again and her heart rate tripled. Her gaze locked with his.

His eyes were a stormy blue, deep and penetrating. The high cheekbones and planes of his face made him seem stern. His eyes narrowed as he studied her from her damp hat to scuffed boots. She hadn't a clue to his thoughts, however, as his expression remained impassive.

She hoped her own thoughts weren't clearly visible on her face. She was attracted to this cowboy.

And that was a complication she didn't want!

"Pleasure, ma'am."

His voice rumbled around them like thunder, deep and dark. When he released her hand, she felt a sense of loss.

"Nice to meet you, Mr. Randall. Unfortunately, I don't have a position open at the moment."

Though for one second she almost considered making one up just for the joy of hiring him.

Summer only, huh? Pity, she wouldn't be here even if she did hire him.

Josh Randall looked like a strong man, not one to waste time or effort. Too bad he hadn't showed up three months ago. Things would change when her brother got home in a few days. If he wanted to hire someone while she was gone, she'd let him make that decision.

She shook her head slowly when she turned back to Bob.

"Marc's coming home in a week or so. I can manage until then."

She looked again at Josh Randall, feeling a shy uncertainty in his presence. He carried himself with a confidence that she found fascinating and appealing. she wished she could offer him a job—and spend some time with him.

But not now. She had plans.

"Sure, Becca, just thought I'd mention it to you. So your brother's finally graduating and returning home."

She nodded, smiling broadly.

"And will I be glad. After Brad Donovan quit last winter, I held off hiring anyone else knowing Marc would be home by June. But it's been tough being down a man."

She looked at Josh. "If you'd been here last February, I'd have taken you on in a heartbeat."

She looked back at the owner of the feed store. "How about Johnson's place, isn't he looking for someone?"

Bob shook his head. "Hired a man from Texas just a week or so ago."

"Sorry," she said, daring to meet Josh's eyes once again.

"If I hear of anything—"

He shook his head. "Thanks, but that's not necessary. If there's nothing open around here I'll be moving on. I'm looking for a short-term hire for the summer. I'll find something. 'Preciate your help, Bob. Good to see you again."

He shook hands with the man, tipped his hat to Becca and strode from the building, the heels of his boots echoing on the wooden floor.

"Wow, he's big," she said, watching him walk away.

"Yep and he's a good man, always a hard worker. He's got some good recommendations from a couple of the big ranches south of here. Even ran his own spread for a while. Something will turn up for him. So what can I do for you, young lady?"

Josh walked out into the sunshine glad to see it'd stopped raining. Resetting his hat firmly on his head, he skirted a muddy pick up truck and headed to his own rig. The horse trailer gleamed silver and maroon in the sparkling light. The rain had washed off every trace of dust.

He heard the muffled stomp of his horses as he approached. They'd had the run of a field yesterday so could stay in the trailer for a few more hours.

Bob had given him the name of a rancher who would let his horses share his corral for the night. He'd grab a bite to eat and then head for the ranch. Once the horses were seen to, he'd look for a motel for himself. Tomorrow he'd head on north. Maybe the next town would have something for him.

Deliberately refusing to think about the woman he'd just

met, he pulled out of the parking lot and headed down Main Street. There had to be a cafe. Ah, there. He parked the double rig on a side street and walked back to the family-style restaurant.

He didn't have the time nor inclination to think about some pretty rancher who'd barely come up to his chin. He had more important things to think about. He'd been looking for work for over a week. Not long by most standards, yet long enough for him to be impatient with the lack of success.

And long enough to wish he'd found another job before quitting the last one.

He didn't want to eat into his savings. He was so close to his goal. A few more months pay and he'd have enough for a down payment on a spread of his own. By fall he hoped he'd be searching the market for a small ranch.

He needed to focus on finding work, not wondering how soft Becca Montgomery's hand felt in his, or how silky her hair might be or what she'd look like in a dress. The jeans she wore clung to her hips snug enough to give him a fine idea of her figure. A bit on the thin side, but still all woman. Her jacket loosely covered her, but he bet she was slender all over.

Scowling, he sat at the counter and ordered coffee.

Becca parked near the center of town. She'd ordered what she needed from Bob, loaded some of the things in the back of the truck after arranging to have the rest delivered. Glancing at her watch, she had plenty of time before her appointment with the lawyer.

Dashing across the street, she ducked into the post office. The postbox for the ranch was large and usually filled with fliers, magazines, and promotional materials, letters to the cowboys who lived on the ranch, as well as bills.

Gathering the day's delivery, she returned to the truck and sat in the cab sifting through the mail, sorting advertisements from bills, journals from catalogs, the letters for her men.

To her surprise, she found a letter addressed to her mixed up in the stack. It was unusual to find a letter for her.

Her stepmother rarely wrote. Usually she called, but even phone calls were few and far between. Becca had no other relatives, except for Marc, away at college, and Suzanne at the ranch. Her friends either texted or sent an email if they didn't call. She didn't expect letters in the mail. Bills, yes, they were always addressed to her.

She studied the envelope for a moment. Her address was typed, there was no return address. Tempted to rip it open, she decided to stretch out the anticipation a bit longer, savor the spark of excitement wondering who'd written her.

She'd grab a cup of coffee at the cafe and read her letter there. Tucking it into her shirt pocket, Becca finished sorting the mail.

Curiosity burned as she tried to think who'd write her. The postmark had been blurred. She could hardly wait to open it, yet deliberately held off. She'd enjoy the anticipation a bit longer.

In a few moments she sat at a booth along the side wall of Carla's Cafe. Her cup of coffee cooling before her. Scanning the cafe upon entering, she'd noticed Josh Randall at the counter, putting away a meal that would have lasted her all day. She nodded in passing, slipping into the booth the waitress indicated.

It was warm and cozy in the cafe. The black-and-white

floor shone around the damp tracks of the customers. The lights gleamed, brightening the back of the café as the sun drenched the front. She reached for her letter. Plenty of time to read it before her appointment.

Glimpsing the signature when she pulled it from the envelope, she realized it was from Marc. Perplexed, she frowned as she began to read.

When she realized exactly what he'd written, she leaned back in the booth, feeling as if she'd been kicked in the chest by a bull. She read the letter again. Her numb fingers let it drift to the table. Her eyes no longer saw the words dancing across the page. She was in shock.

He wasn't coming back.

She couldn't believe it.

For years she had planned on the day he'd graduate from college and return to help run the ranch.

She'd scrimped and saved, gone without any vacations she might have taken in order to keep things running on the ranch. Passed up personal opportunities in order to keep her family together. Stayed on the ranch and done everything she could until Marc could join her and shoulder some of the burden.

And now he calmly writes to say he wasn't coming back!

For a moment her eyes filled with tears. She'd been planning on so much--dependent on Marc's taking over and letting her have some time away from the ranch, away from Wyoming. A chance to see something else of the world beside the Wind River Range.

Ironically, she'd been on her way to the lawyer's to arrange to transfer part ownership of the ranch to Marc. It was to have been a surprise graduation gift. A gift of love to her brother.

Instead, he wasn't returning. He planned to go to California.

She couldn't take it in. All this time she thought—

"Problem?"

The deep, sexy voice sounded familiar. Slowly Becca raised her gaze. She blinked the tears away and Josh Randall came into focus, standing by the booth, looking at her with some concern.

She shook her head, then nodded. "I—" She swallowed hard. "No, no problem. I just had a bit of bad news." She gestured to the letter.

Josh slid into the bench, opposite her. "Anything I can do?"

She shook her head. Carefully folding the letter, she slipped it back into the envelope staring at it. She still couldn't believe it.

Why hadn't Marc said anything to her before? Why had he hidden the fact he was taking computer courses, not the agricultural ones she thought he was studying?

Why had he let her believe all along that he'd be returning to the ranch when he obviously never intended to do so? He knew she was counting on his return.

She felt betrayed, hurt, stunned.

Suddenly anger washed through her, hot and strengthening. She especially thought it cowardly to write and not even call or show up to tell her in person.

She looked up and met Josh's eyes. "Sometimes you think you know someone and it's a bit of a shock when you discover you hadn't a clue."

He looked startled. "True."

"Things have changed, Mr. Randall. I'm looking for a hand, after all. My brother won't be coming next week."

His eyes flickered to the letter, back to her. "Wants a fling after graduation?" he guessed.

"Not coming back at all, according to the letter."

She couldn't keep the hurt from her tone, but she refused to let it stop her from functioning. She'd had other setbacks and overcome them, she'd manage with this one, as well.

She just needed a little time. Time and some sort of explanation from Marc beyond his paltry letter. He could have come home and told her face-to-face.

He could at least have called!

She thought of the travel brochures on her desk. Of the plans she'd outlined, the places she wanted to visit. She'd hoped to leave a week or two after he came home.

Now those plans were dashed.

First things first, however. "Still interested in a job?" she asked.

"Depends."

He pushed the brim of his hat back and slouched a bit on the bench. His long legs stretched beneath the table near hers. His eyes held Becca's.

"Bob Mason didn't get much of a chance to tell you what I'm looking for. I'm not just a regular cowhand. I'm looking to ramrod a place. Give the owner some time off so to speak. Shoulder some of the administrative burden as well as management. But only for a few months. By the end of the summer I'll be leaving. I need to be up front and clear about that."

"I manage the ranch myself, I don't need a foreman," she said.

The disappointment she felt was way out of proportion. She'd just met Josh Randall, she couldn't be disappointed he wasn't interested in a job on the Lazy M.

She was suffering from Marc's defection, that was all.

He nodded. "Then I guess I'll be heading north. I'm sorry the news hit you so hard."

Becca stared at him for a long moment, reluctant to have the conversation end. Reluctant to bid farewell to the stranger. An idea gleamed.

It was impossible.

Wait, she needed to examine it for a second.

It might work.

Dare she try?

Dare she grab out with both hands and think of herself at this late date? Or was she overreacting to Marc's letter?

Josh didn't move. He watched her as she appeared to be thinking deeply about something. The expressions chasing around her face were priceless. He watched as the color washed into her cheeks and then realized how pale she'd been. He wondered what had been in the letter, wondered why her brother wasn't returning. Wondered how it would be to work with her.

With her hat off he could see her hair was that rich chestnut color that gleamed with golden highlights in the sun, pulled back from her face in a functional ponytail at the base of her neck.

He wondered how long and thick it was. What it would look like unconfined? Was it as silky as it looked? She wore no makeup, her gray eyes were large and darkly lashed. She was thin, not too tall. He liked women with a bit more in the curves department, but she was pretty, in a fresh, open, girl-next-door kind of way.

He frowned and mentally pulled in the reins. He had no intention of getting tangled up with any woman for a long time to come. If ever again. And he certainly knew better than to trust a rancher with more land than manpower. He wanted a job that gave him the scope to do what he did best, but not at the cost he'd paid once before.

And he only wanted a job for as long as it took to get the rest of the money he needed to buy a place of his own.

Becca never did impulsive things. She examined all aspects of a situation before proceeding. Yet she didn't have the luxury of the time. If she didn't speak up in the next few minutes, Josh Randall would head out of town and she'd have lost the opportunity.

Maybe her only opportunity to take some of those trips she wanted so badly.

"Mr. Randall—" she began.

"Josh," he corrected.

"Josh, then. I might be interested in a foreman after all. I can afford it now that I no longer have to pay college costs. And I could sure use a break."

She hadn't left the ranch, except to visit town, in the six years since her father died. She'd put all of her dreams and hopes on hold as she struggled to hold on to the place, to make a home for her brother and sister.

Her brother obviously didn't feel it important enough to even come home and talk to her. After supporting him for years, he sent a letter.

Maybe it was time to do something for herself, if only

have someone shoulder the burden with her.

"Bob said you know plenty about ranching," she said.

He signaled the waitress for another cup of coffee. When he had his mug, he looked into the dark brew as if looking for the words.

"I was raised on a ranch in Colorado. Did some rodeoing when I was a kid. Then I worked spreads from Cripple Creek to Bozeman. A few years ago I—"

He hesitated, picked up his cup and took a sip.

"Acquired part interest in a ranch. Lost it last year. I tried working this past year as a regular hand, but found I don't deal well with stupidity of some of the managers. I need to run things."

She understood. After running the Lazy M for six years, she'd wondered a few times if she'd be able to share the task with Marc.

Now that was no longer a worry.

Could she relinquish some of the day-to-day control to someone else? A stranger?

At least as owner she'd retain final say.

And if it worked out, she could take at least one of the trips she planned.

"Financial problems?" she asked sympathetically. She couldn't imagine what it would be like to lose the Lazy M.

He looked at her.

"Is that why you lost your ranch?"

"Nope. Divorce." Bitterness laced his tone.

Surprised, Becca didn't know what to say. She waited a moment.

"I'll want to think about this a bit more. But I could use

the help at the ranch and maybe a foreman's just what I need."

She took a deep breath. She hadn't told anyone of her dreams in a long time. But for some reason they crowded around, anxious to be released. She hadn't begrudged Marc the money for college. Even though it meant postponing her own plans. But she had been counting on his help, hoped to at last realize some of her own dreams.

She met Josh's calm gaze.

"I've always wanted to travel. To take some time and go see more of the world. If things work out, you could run the ranch for me for the summer and I could take off for a while," she said hesitantly.

He nodded.

"If you start today, we could have a trial period. I'd want to check references. You could see what the Lazy M is like. If in a couple of weeks we both still feel the same way, we can make it permanent," she offered.

It wasn't that Bob Mason's recommendation wasn't enough. Becca'd feel more comfortable if she had more than one person tell her this man would work out.

"That suits me," he said gravely. "You understand it's not permanent. Only for the summer."

"Summer ends September 21, would you stay until then?"

He hesitated a moment, then nodded.

She offered her hand and when his larger one closed over hers, she felt a tingling shimmer of physical awareness unlike anything she'd experienced. Perplexed, she glanced at their clasped hands. The handshake was brief, as the one in the feed and grain had been. Yet the sensations lingered.

15

"Ready to leave?" he asked.

"I have to make a quick phone call to cancel an appointment that's no longer necessary and I'll be ready. You can follow me to the ranch."

Becca dropped some money on the table and scooted out of the booth. It didn't take long to cancel the meeting with her lawyer.

Before she knew it, she led the way out of town, the big silver-and-maroon truck and horse trailer right behind her.

Becca looked in the rear view mirror, wondering about her new foreman. She had a million questions she wanted answered, most centering around his brief statement about losing his ranch. To divorce. She shivered.

She'd hate to lose the Lazy M. It had been her home all her life. She loved every inch of the place. Had Josh loved his ranch? Had he explored all the boundaries, every draw and arroyo? Had he known every tree, every pond, every blade of grass?

And had he still loved his wife when they divorced?

The thought came unbidden. She glanced behind her again, then focused on the road ahead. It wasn't any of her business. She hired a foreman. All she had to worry about was if he did the job well.

Was he easy to live with? He looked hard, intense. Did he ever laugh and joke around? What did he do for fun?

"Stop it," she admonished herself. "Think of something else."

Right, like Marc. How could he have lied to her for four years? How could he have let her plan on his help, count on his returning, when he'd known all along he didn't plan to return to the ranch. He hadn't majored in agriculture, but computer science, according to today's letter. And now he had a job offer in California.

Blast it all! She'd worked long and hard to put him through school, made do without so he could get the education she'd have killed for.

And he repaid her like this.

Anger flared so strong she had a hard time seeing straight.

A toot of the horn behind her warned her she was all over the road. Relaxing her grip on the steering wheel, she concentrated on driving.

Time enough to rant and rave at her brother's perfidy.

Stepbrother, she reminded herself.

The young hellion who hadn't wanted to move to the ranch when his mother married her father. Yet over the years, Becca thought he'd changed his mind. Looking back she could be excused for thinking that. He'd said he loved the ranch more than once. And over the four years of school he'd never once suggested anything to lead her to believe he wasn't returning.

Josh followed Becca, wondering what she was doing when she began to weave across the road. He sounded his horn. Probably upset about her brother's letter, he concluded.

Maybe she was crying and couldn't see. Bad situation. He'd like to meet the man, see what kind of coward wrote to say he wasn't coming home. He couldn't deliver the news in person?

Not that it was any of his business. He wanted a job, pure and simple. He planned to save as much of his pay as he could, until he could afford to buy a spread of his own.

The next time he owned a ranch, it'd be his free and clear. No joint ownership. No partnerships. Solely his.

And if he was ever foolish enough to consider marriage again, he'd lock everything up so tight legally, nothing would slip through if the marriage ended.

Not that he planned on another marriage. Once was enough. More than enough, as it turned out.

And when he got a place of his own, he'd only hire bachelors. No women around to cause trouble. He'd raise his horses, run a few head of cattle, and enjoy life.

The driveway from the road was short and in only seconds he saw the two-story ranch house. Beyond sat the rest of the buildings comprising the Lazy M.

Becca drove past the house and straight to the barn, Josh still behind her. Slowly she surveyed the large structure. She was glad Josh got to see the ranch first in the sunshine. Everything was freshly painted, repaired and in top-notch shape.

She was extremely proud of the Lazy M. Her father had been a great rancher and she tried her best to follow in his footsteps.

Some days, however, she just didn't know if she had what it took for the long haul. Sometimes she got so tired. And there was so much more she wanted from life than staying on the Lazy M.

There were places to see outside of Wyoming—historic sites and famous ones; the sea and the wide rushing rivers and skyscrapers that towered over city canyons. She wanted to explore New York and lie on the beach in Florida. She wanted to see the Alamo and the Liberty Bell. She wanted to surf in Hawaii and spot whales in Puget Sound.

She didn't want to be a rancher all her life.

Sighing, Becca cut the engine. She'd see how Josh worked out. If things went well, maybe she could take a few of her trips. If only for the summer.

Josh pulled up beside her and scanned the yard, neat, clean, well-repaired. She ran a good spread.

He opened the door and stepped out into the yard. Rotating his shoulders to loosen them, he headed to the rear of the horse trailer. Becca was already there.

"I have one stall and the corral."

She'd spotted the two horses.

"The corral will be fine for Bonnie. Rampage will use the stall."

He unfastened the lever, released the ramp and slowly lowered it to the ground.

Hopping inside, he began to back out the sorrel filly.

"She's a beauty," Becca commented from the corral gate.

As he approached, she swung it open wide enough for the horse to move inside. Josh let her go and joined Becca as she swung the gate closed. There were two other horses in the corral watching the newcomer.

"I want to breed the two of them when she comes into season," he said as his mare wandered to the water trough and began to drink.

"So the other one's a stallion?" she asked with a frown. "How wild is he?"

Josh's eyes softened in amusement.

Becca watched, fascinated by the change. They became a deep blue, like a mountain lake, or the sky over Wyoming on a clear, sunny summer's day. Even the harsh angles of his face seem to soften just a mite.

"He's as gentle as a lamb, unless he's around a mare in season. The rest of the time, he's a fine cutting horse. We've won a few prizes."

She glanced at the big silver buckle at his narrow waist. A prize for bronc riding at some rodeo. She suspected Josh Randall had won more than a few events. She'd like to find out more, but later. He might not even stay. For some reason that thought disturbed her.

The barn's double doors stood wide and Becca walked inside. It was dry and almost warm. The high loft was still stacked with bales of hay from last season, the dirt in the center of the building hard-packed and swept clean. The stalls that lined the walkway contained an assortment of horses, a bay, two chestnuts, and an Appaloosa.

Becca walked to the end stall and swung the gate open. When Josh settled his horse, she turned and headed out.

"I'll show you the bunkhouse. You can unpack and then join me for lunch at the house. I'll go over as much as I can today. If the rain holds off, we can take a ride later. But frankly, I've been out in the rain for the last three days and so if it starts again, if I don't have to go today, I don't want to."

He nodded. She needed him. Things would work out.

And he didn't need to see the spread today. He'd be here for a while.

Fifteen minutes later Becca drove her pickup to the back of the house. She stepped into the back porch and used the boot jack to remove her boots. Shrugging out of her jacket, she hung it on a hook. In her stocking feet she entered the warm kitchen, dropping the stack of mail on the large table. She'd left the cowboys mail at the bunk house when showing

Josh which room would be his.

"Suzanne?" she called.

Chili bubbled on the stove. The aroma called to Becca and she walked over to scoop up a spoonful. It was hot. Blowing on it to cool, she waited impatiently.

She was hungry, mad, confused and tired.

She'd take a hot shower and change into dry clothes before lunch. After that she'd be tied up with Josh all afternoon. Time enough tonight to sort out what she was going to do about Marc. If anything.

"Hi, Becca. Don't eat that, it has to cook a little longer."

Tall, blond, stylishly dressed, Suzanne Cannon sauntered into the kitchen and leaned against the counter, studying her stepsister.

"Tastes good now."

Becca sampled the chili, dropped the spoon into the sink.

"I planned to eat around one. I thought you'd be gone longer. You said this morning—"

"Things changed. I hired a new man. He'll eat lunch with us and I told him to be here at twelve-thirty."

Suzanne sighed. "Another rough cowboy? Can't he eat at the bunkhouse?"

"There's no one there. The others are out checking on the cattle and the fencing. Besides, he's not a rough cowboy. He's my new foreman."

"What?" Suzanne stared at Becca. "What about Marc?"

Becca fished out the letter and handed it to her sister. "That's what about Marc. I'm going to take a shower. I'll be down in a half hour."

Two

Josh knocked at the back door. He didn't know if he was expected to enter or wait to be admitted. Wouldn't hurt to wait, at least the first time.

Becca opened the door. "Come in. If your boots are muddy, leave them on the porch."

He complied, saw her jacket on a hook and placed his beside it. He stepped inside the warm kitchen in his thick socks, the smell of chili started the saliva flowing.

He wondered if he was expected to eat his future meals with his boss or the men in the bunkhouse. If the food was as good as it smelled, he wanted to eat here.

"Josh, this is my sister, Suzanne Cannon. Suzanne, Josh Randall, our new foreman."

Becca made the introductions casually as she dished chili into bowls.

"Well, hello, there. Becca, fix an extra-large bowl for this one, he looks like he needs a lot to keep him going."

Suzanne smiled up at Josh, her eyes alight with laughter and flirtation. He watched her cross the room in a long-legged walk that was provocative as could be. She was obviously out to see what she could get.

He knew her type. She reminded him of Tiff. Holding

out her hand, she held his longer than necessary, reluctant to release him when he pulled away.

He'd have to watch her, she could prove to be a handful.

Josh's eyes flickered between her and Becca. No family resemblance at all. Suzanne was tall and blond. Her hair curled and waved around her face, looking as if she'd just come from bed. Her makeup was skillfully applied—not for her the girl-next-door look. She was amply endowed in all the right places, aware of her charms and ready to practice at a moment's notice.

Josh sat where Becca indicated, noticing Suzanne's jeans were new, designer label and all. She had on fancy running shoes and a silk shirt.

A silk shirt on a working ranch? He shook his head.

But he couldn't help comparing her with Becca. The snug jeans covering that little lady's legs were worn and faded. Her shirt was a practical cotton, long sleeves rolled up to her elbows. Her hair was pulled back in a ponytail, neat, tidy, functional.

And a whole lot more appealing than her fancy sister.

He waited until Becca began to eat then tasted his own chili. Best he'd had in a while.

"Where are you from, Josh, and what brings you to the Wind River area?" Suzanne asked, leaning forward across the table, her eyes gazing at him as if she couldn't wait to hear his answer.

Josh looked at her. "I'm from Colorado, originally. Cheyenne most recently."

His words were brief, succinct. He hadn't hired on to flirt with the owner's sister.

"And you've come to the ranch to work as foreman. I

didn't even know Becca was looking for someone. She's always done all the work herself. She's so industrious. And knows tons about ranching. Of course, she was born and raised here on the ranch. I've only lived here for the last ten years or so after my mom married her dad. Before that we lived in Denver. It's such a beautiful city. If you're from Colorado, you must know Denver."

He nodded.

"Are you from there?" she persisted, smiling provocatively.

Her entire attention focused upon him as if he were the most important thing in her life.

Becca watched, fascinated. Suzanne had always been able to wrap the men around her little finger. Her feminine air appealed to the rough, strong men that worked the ranches in central Wyoming. Her golden beauty ensnared them, had them dreaming fantasies with the lovely woman at the center.

But Suzanne was fickle. She played around, never satisfied, always wanting more.

Curious to see how long it would be before Josh succumbed, Becca watched in resignation. How would it be to have a man feel strongly about her?

She rather thought she'd like it, but didn't have a chance as long as they saw Suzanne first.

"I've visited Denver. We lived in Cripple Creek," Josh replied.

"Oh, an old gold mining town. How romantic. I love history, don't you? There's not much around here, except for South Pass where the wagons cut through on their way to Oregon. Still, just riding through the hills gives me the feeling of the old Indians who once roamed the range, the early settlers." Suzanne smiled ingeniously.

Josh continued eating the chili. He saw through the ploys of the oh-so-charming young woman. She was a flirt, pure and simple.

He glanced at Becca, startled to find her speculative gaze on him.

"Do you share your sister's love for history?" he asked, curious about his new boss.

He really wanted to ask her about the setup. Despite her insistence on calling Marc and Suzanne brother and sister, the last names and the comment Suzanne made about her mother marrying Becca's father indicated they weren't related by blood.

Yet they appeared to have a close family tie, which made the brother's defection all the more puzzling.

She shrugged. "I enjoy history, but I don't have the time to get caught up in romanticizing about it as Suzanne does."

"Becca doesn't have many interests beside the ranch," Suzanne said petulantly.

"I do, but I rarely have the time to indulge myself," Becca replied without rancor.

"Work, work, work. What would you do if you didn't have the ranch to fuss over?" Suzanne quipped, turning back to Josh. "What do you like to do on your off time, cowboy?" she asked provocatively.

"Depends on where I am and who I'm with," he replied.

"There's a place in town that has a hot band. We could go in one night—"

"Suzanne!"

Becca cringed with embarrassment at her sister's

behavior even though Suzanne showed no such shame. "Josh is here to work, not entertain you."

"I'll let you know," Josh said, pushing his empty bowl away and resting his folded arms on the table's edge. "But first I have to come up to scratch on my job. Wouldn't want my new boss to fire me for dereliction of duty."

"Don't let her work you to death. Honestly, that's all she does," Suzanne repeated, with a glare at Becca.

"And if I didn't, who would?" Becca asked, the anger over Marc's betrayal simmering just below the surface.

She didn't need a second attack from her sister.

"It'd get done or it wouldn't. If not, I doubt the world would end," Suzanne said.

"Maybe the world as a whole wouldn't, but yours would, Suzanne, dear. Money doesn't grow on trees, you know."

"No, it grows on cattle, and God knows we have plenty of those creatures. You know, Becca, I'll be twenty-one in two more weeks."

"Yes, I know that. We'll have a party."

"I don't want a party. What I want is my share of the ranch."

Becca stared at Suzanne as if she'd never seen her before. "What do you mean, you want your share?"

A sense of foreboding crept over Becca. A feeling of disorientation simmered. Was the entire world going amok?

"I want you to buy me out. You don't think I'm planning to bury myself here forever, do you? I should have gone with Mom when she first left. Now she's married to that stodgy stockbroker and made it clear that I'd be a fifth wheel. So I need some money, obviously, to make it on my own."

"This is your home, Suzanne. If you don't want to do

the housework and cooking, maybe you could find a job in town."

Suzanne slanted her gaze to Josh, dismissing him, and returning to meet Becca's eyes. "No offense, Becca, but I want more in my life than to spend it on a ranch like you do." She stood. "I've had it with this blasted place. I certainly don't want to stay here and get a job in town. Once I'm twenty-one, I want money that's due me. I'm getting out of Wyoming and seeing some of the world!"

She gathered the dirty dishes and dumped them into the sink with a clatter.

Becca swallowed hard. She wished she could go back to bed and start the day over. She'd never experienced so many blows at one time.

She'd known that Suzanne was dissatisfied with things lately, but not that she'd been harboring plans to leave after her birthday.

Or that she thought she could just demand a sum of money to speed her on her way.

"You want to tell me about the setup here?" Josh asked over the sound of rushing water.

Becca nodded, feeling dazed and numb.

"We can talk in the office. Thanks for lunch, Suzanne. Your chili can't be beat."

Suzanne nodded, but concentrated on the dishes, saying nothing.

Becca sank into the chair behind the old desk in the office with some relief. At least here she knew where she stood. Longing for a few moments to herself to assimilate the shocking surprises she'd experienced, she knew she needed to get business out of the way first.

Josh roamed around the room while Becca watched him. He seemed to bring a breath of fresh air into the place, his energy infectious. Studying him, she became conscious of his masculinity.

Something within her responded as she felt warmth and uncertainty spread. She hadn't been attracted to a man in many years. She tried to be friendly with the men who worked for her, had several friends among the neighboring ranches, but since her father's death, no one had touched her imagination or romantic inclinations.

Not that Josh had, either, she quickly assured herself. She was simply intrigued by him.

He looked at her, his dark blue eyes piercing as if he could see deep within her. She met his gaze without wavering, but wanted to glance away, longed to give in to the shyness that seemed to grip her at his look and shelter herself from his assessment.

He sat opposite her, filling the chair, his broad shoulders looking capable of any task set before him. He rested one ankle on the knee of his other leg, rested his hand on his bent knee. His fingers were blunt-tipped, his palms large.

Becca remembered the hard calluses that she'd felt when they shook hands. For a startling moment she wondered what those fingertips would feel like against other parts of her body.

A tendril of warmth stirred, spread. Good grief, she refused to act like a love-starved girl giddy with a crush on some heartthrob. And Josh would never fill the role as heartthrob. He was too roughly masculine, too virile—as rugged as the Wyoming mountains.

For the first time in six years Becca wished she looked

different. Wished her hair curled softly around her face as Suzanne's did. Wished she'd taken time to put on a dash of makeup after her shower. Her eyes were nice. With a bit of trouble, they became her best feature. She could have at least put on newer clothes.

With a rueful glance down at the faded jeans, the old serviceable shirt, she sighed. She wasn't here to entice a cowboy, no matter how sexy she found him. She was here to work.

Work, work, work. Just as Suzanne had said.

What Suzanne ignored was the fact that if Becca didn't work hard, they wouldn't enjoy the life-style they did. Marc could not have gone to college, all expenses paid. His mother had been clear she wasn't footing the bill.

Suzanne couldn't indulge herself with designer clothes and all the jewelry she loved.

Neither had said no to the money Becca's hard work produced.

Afraid to continue her thoughts lest she give way to self-pity, she shook off the gloom. Time enough later to decide what she was going to do.

Right now, she had a new foreman to deal with.

She reached into the second drawer and drew forth a folded map, spreading it out on the desk. Rising to lean over it, too short to see it all from her chair, she beckoned Josh closer.

"This is the Lazy M," she began.

Two hours later Josh mounted Rampage and rode out of the barn. The horizon was dark and ominous, threatening more rain as the row of clouds enveloped the late afternoon sun. The ground was soft and soggy underfoot, but the big stallion didn't let it bother him. His head held high, his step prancing and playful, he lunged against the bit, the desire to run evident.

"Go, boy. We'll get the kinks out and then settle down to explore."

Josh gave him his head and they raced across the range. Attentive to the landmarks and fields rushing by, Josh still had time to think about his new job.

And his new boss.

He liked Becca. She seemed sensible, unlike her flirty sister who acted as if she thought men existed solely to pay her court. Becca knew her business. She'd shown him the ranch boundaries, commented on the different problems they faced; talked about the cattle she ran. Her ideas were sound, some innovative.

And she sure as goodness needed someone else to help shoulder the burden.

No wonder Suzanne thought she worked hard all the time. She had to in order to keep the place afloat.

He reviewed their meeting as he let his horse run the kinks out. When he'd mentioned how well the ranch seemed to be doing, her face had glowed with pride.

"Do you think so?" Becca asked.

"Looks like you're doing a fine job. Not easy, either, with the size of the spread."

"My dad left it to me when he died. I'm really just sort of maintaining it along the lines he ran it," she confided.

"Then he set it up well. No trouble with hiring good hands?"

"Only once, when he found out he'd have to work for a woman." She glanced up and smiled impishly. "That should change. I expect you're man enough for any cowboy that ever set foot on the range."

Josh almost caught his breath at her grin. It changed her entire face and almost knocked his socks off. She was adorable when she smiled. Not a raving beauty like her sister, but a warm, lovely woman.

"What is it you want from me, Becca?" he asked, instinctively drawing back from that smile.

Wary at any show of friendliness. He wouldn't forget Tiffany and how their relationship started.

Becca sat down in her chair and leaned back. "Actually I don't know. I'm tired, Josh. I work hard every day and there're still so many things to do. I'd hoped when Marc came back he'd take some of the burden. I don't know how long I can continue. What can you do to help me?"

"I can run the place for you, if that's what you want. You can oversee the books once a month, and do what you want the rest of the time. And as well as you've done, I think I can increase your income this year by close to ten percent."

She stared at him for a long time, but he knew she didn't see him. Her gaze was slightly unfocused and he'd wanted to know what she thought about.

"Becca?" he asked.

"I had to leave school when my father died. I loved college. It was the first time I'd been away from the ranch for any length of time. It was so much fun. I met girls from different backgrounds. I dated boys who'd never seen a horse, much less worked cattle. I learned so much beyond the basics of the classrooms." She smiled sadly and sighed.

"One day I'd like to go back to school."

"And study what?"

She shrugged. "I don't know. I'd planned to major in business when I first started college. Of course I thought my father would be around for another thirty years, so I thought I could go somewhere else and work in another field for a while."

"I'm surprised your father didn't expect Marc to run the ranch."

She looked up. Hesitating only a moment, she explained. "Suzanne and Marc aren't his children. He married Eileen when her kids were ten and eleven. That's what Suzanne meant when she said she'd only lived here for ten years."

"Where's her mother?"

"When my father died, she left. She didn't really like the ranch, only my father. A couple of years ago she remarried."

"She left her children here, for you to raise?"

"I didn't mind. They are my brother and sister, after all."

He studied the petite woman, wondering if the two other people involved appreciated the extra worry and work they caused a young girl.

"How old were you when your father died?" he asked abruptly. It wasn't his business, but he found his curiosity growing. He wanted to find out more about her. She was as different from his ex-wife Tiffany as any woman he'd met.

Not that he dare trust her, he'd learned that lesson well. But he was intrigued.

"Twenty."

"And Marc and Suzanne?"

Becca looked puzzled. "Marc was sixteen and Suzanne fifteen, why?"

"Their mother should have taken them with her if she didn't want to remain on the ranch."

"I wouldn't have had any family left if they'd gone with Eileen. I was glad they stayed."

"It couldn't have been easy."

She smiled and shook her head. "Are teenagers ever easy? But they're family. All I have left."

"Steps."

The smile dropped from her face and anger flared. "They are my family. End of discussion. I suggest you remember that in the future."

Josh drew the horse into a walk, almost smiling at the memory of Becca flaring up when he dare insinuate her family wasn't as close as she wanted to believe.

She reminded him of a little kitten. He could almost see her arch her back and flash tiny claws. She'd have to have spirit to carry this ranch. It was big and sprawling and would take iron determination and hard work to keep it successful.

He wouldn't mind working here until he saved enough to buy his own place. And with the wages Becca offered, that might come sooner than he thought. In the meantime, he'd see what he could do to ease the burdens of the woman who'd given him the job.

Becca leaned back in her chair and gazed out the window. She should have gone with Josh. She should have shown him around the ranch, introduced him to the men. She should have done all that, but he'd said he'd manage on his own. And she let him.

As she was going to let him take over some aspects of the ranch.

She astonished herself.

Though the entire day itself had been astonishing. First her very physical attraction to the stranger in the feed store. Normally she didn't notice men, so her reaction with Josh surprised her.

Marc's letter and Suzanne's startling comment both had been totally unexpected. Becca knew she had to make some hard decisions in the next couple of days.

But today she couldn't muster the energy.

Instead she thought about Josh. He liked what she'd done with the ranch. There were several suggestions he made about mustering the herd for the spring sale that she'd never have thought of. It came from years more experience, she knew. But for a moment she felt almost insufficient to the task ahead.

How old was he? She'd have to ask. He looked around thirty, but she wasn't good at judging ages.

Divorced, he'd said. So he was single.

And after Suzanne's flirting at lunch, probably ready to take her up on her offer to go dancing.

Becca frowned. She wished Suzanne hadn't made her play. Couldn't she leave at least one man alone? She'd already gone out with every man on the place, a couple more than once.

Yet she just played the field. Suzanne was too young to get serious about anyone. And after her comments at lunch, Becca knew her sister wouldn't set her sights on a cowboy, no matter how sexy.

Becca sighed and folded the map, dissatisfied with her

thoughts. She wasn't jealous precisely, she only wished Suzanne would leave Josh alone. Becca could use a friend right about now and her new foreman would be her first choice.

She paused, startled with the thought.

Why not her sister? Or one of her school friends, or even one or two of the men who'd worked the ranch since her father's time?

Why Josh Randall, the man she'd met only a few hours ago?

Slowly she wandered up to her room. It was close to supper time. She wanted to go to the bunkhouse and make sure all the ranch hands met Josh and knew he had her full confidence as her new foreman.

She pulled out a new pair of jeans and quickly changed. Pulling on a bright yellow sweater, she brushed her hair until it shone, letting it fall to her shoulders. Sparingly she touched her lashes with dark mascara. She looked as nice as she got. Nothing to compare with Suzanne, but then, she wasn't competing. She just wanted to spruce up a bit before meeting with the men.

"Well, well, aren't we all dolled up," Suzanne drawled when Becca entered the kitchen a few minutes later.

"Don't be silly. I just put on a sweater. It's cool this afternoon."

"And where are you going?"

"Down to the bunkhouse. I want to make sure everyone knows I've hired Josh as foreman and that he's in charge now."

Suzanne narrowed her eyes. "Why? Becca, honestly, you've managed this place fine since your father died. Why hire a foreman? I bet you're paying him more than you're paying any of the other ranch hands. Why the big change?"

"I expected Marc to help out. I've been holding on since my father died expecting Marc to take on half the responsibility when he graduated. Now he's out of the picture."

"Seems to me you rushed right into hiring the first man you saw after you got the letter. Are you sure there isn't more to it? I haven't seen you get so dressed up in years," Suzanne said slyly.

"Dressed up? For heaven's sake, Suzanne, I'm wearing jeans and a sweater!"

Her sister ran her gaze over her, met Becca's eyes.

"The jeans are new and tight. Showing off how slender you really are. The sweater brings color to your cheeks. And your hair is loose, instead of in its normal ponytail. And correct me if I'm wrong, but I think I see makeup."

Becca felt heat sting her cheeks. She didn't need this. Was she making a fool of herself? Maybe she should go back to her room and wash her face and put back on the faded worn jeans she'd worn earlier.

"I'll be back for dinner," she snapped instead.

Storming out onto the porch, she spotted her muddy boots. Some picture she was going to make, clopping in the bunkhouse mired in mud.

Scraping off the worst, she slipped her feet into the boots and stormed out to the truck. No sense trudging through the muck for the distance to the bunkhouse, she thought as she opened the door to the truck.

The wind gusted, swirling around her as she dashed from the truck to the bunkhouse door, blowing her hair every which way. She should have worn it in the ponytail, she thought in disgust, brushing the tangle of hair off her face as she stepped inside.

Josh lounged in the sofa of the communal living room talking with a couple of the men. Down the long hall to the left, each cowboy had a small bedroom containing a bed, chest of drawers and chair. The large communal room contained tables for cards and games, a big screen TV, sofas and chairs for reading and a makeshift bar along one wall that carried a variety of soft drinks.

Becca didn't believe in providing hard liquor to her men. They found enough of that on their trips into town.

His legs were stretched out in front of him, crossed at the ankles. His thumbs were tucked in behind his belt buckle as he leaned back on the sofa cushions, his head rested on the top, lazily turned toward the other men. At her entrance, he glanced over to the door.

For a moment Becca's eyes locked with his. She thought he was going to smile, but instead he rose to his feet and walked toward her in a lazy, lanky gait. Like a sleek cat ambling over to check out something of interest.

Did she interest him?

"I just came to see if you had everything you needed," Becca said breathlessly.

She couldn't take her eyes from his. She felt shy, suddenly uncertain, and didn't like the feeling at all.

"I think I've got all I need. I met the men and took a good look at the Herefords you're running."

He reached out and tucked a strand of hair behind her ear, his finger igniting a blaze against her skin.

She caught her breath.

"Tomorrow I'll check out the mixed breeds. Jason over there was telling me more about the spring sale you and I discussed."

She nodded, unable to speak. She still felt the tingling patch on her skin where he touched her. She wanted to step back, gain a little distance, move away from the enticing man who stood so close she couldn't think.

But the door was behind her, and he stood in front of her, and there was no place to go if she didn't want to look like an idiot darting away.

She cleared her throat. "You met all the men?"

"Yes. You've got a good crew."

"We do," she corrected, wildly trying to come up with a conversation gambit.

She'd never felt so tongue-tied in her life. Why? Just because he brushed back her hair? Just because his eyes were deep and dark and mysterious? Just because he fed her sense of femininity like no other?

"Dinner's up," a voice called from the dining room.

"Are you going to eat with us?" he asked, his voice low, gentle.

"I'm sure Suzanne has fixed something."

She wanted to stay. She wanted to talk to Josh some more. Wanted to see how her men reacted to his arrival.

"There's the phone over there, call her and tell her you're staying."

Becca nodded and slowly stepped around him.

Josh turned to watch her as she walked to the phone. She grinned at Jason as he rose from his chair.

"Tell Mike I might be staying for dinner."

The cowboy smiled and nodded as he hurried from the

room. Aware of Josh's regard, Becca's fingers shook slightly as she dialed the house number.

"Suzanne? I'm staying here for dinner."

"You could have told me on the way out."

"I didn't know then."

"Right. That's why you're all dolled up." Her tone was scathing.

"I'll be home before too late."

"Don't wake me up if I'm already in bed." Suzanne slammed down the receiver.

Becca replaced hers and turned back to Josh. "So tell me, how did the rest of the ranch measure up?"

"It looks good. But there are a couple of areas that need some work because of last winter's snow. Maybe tomorrow we could discuss it. If you ride out with me, I can show you."

"I'd like that."

Three

Dinner was fun. For the first time in years, Becca sat with the ranch hands and simply enjoyed herself. She didn't feel constrained to set an example as boss. Didn't feel the normal wall between them that she so often felt after her father died.

And she owed it to Josh. He made dinner a delight. Yet she wasn't sure how.

He hadn't talked much, just asked a question here and there. But the questions had sparked conversation in the men and in herself. They reminisced about earlier years on the ranch. Most of the men had been there when her father was alive and spoke highly of him.

They teased each other over past events and bragged about their part in the ranch.

Becca grew aware of Josh's gaze on her during the meal. Every time she looked at him, she met his eyes. She knew he watched her. Why? It was disturbing. It was exciting. She longed to spend a few minutes with him alone, away from the other cowboys, to talk about something other than the ranch. But there didn't seem to be a chance.

Finally dinner ended. The men ambled into the communal room and switched on the TV.

"Did you want to discuss those changes now?" she asked, hoping for an opening with Josh.

"Nope. Tomorrow's fine. Don't tell me Suzanne's right, you work all the time?"

She flushed slightly, and shrugged.

It'd been years since she'd been on a date. She had no endless wealth of social chitchat like Suzanne possessed. Becca longed to talk to Josh, to entertain him, to make him aware of her as a woman. But she hadn't the words. She found herself much more comfortable talking with men about ranching.

"I guess I'll head for home," she said, one of the last to leave the dining room table.

"I'll see you back," Josh said quickly.

Too quickly, she thought. He was probably anxious to be shed of his boss so he could relax. She shouldn't have stayed for dinner.

"No need. I drove the truck over. I didn't want to mess with all the mud," Becca said as they left the warm bunkhouse.

The wind swirled around, tossing her hair in her face, sweeping the warmth away, a chill settling around her shoulders. She brushed back her hair, shivering slightly in the cold air. The sky was completely gray. It'd be full dark soon.

"Come with me to check on Rampage. I want to make sure he's settled for the night," Josh said, his hand at the small of her back, turning her gently toward the barn.

Becca leaned against the warmth of his hand. Tingling sensations shimmered deep inside her. She felt sheltered, almost cherished, with the large man at her side.

She prided herself on being strong, on having survived

41

since her father's death in a predominantly man's field. Yet she relished the feminine feeling she experienced walking beside Josh.

When they entered the barn, she flicked on the lights, the soft glow of the bulbs filled the barn.

Tugging her hair back, she wished she'd resisted the urge to let her hair free.

"I should have tied it in a ponytail. It's a mess," she murmured, combing her fingers through the tangled swirls.

Josh shook his head. "I'm glad you didn't. It looked pretty at dinner. In fact, you look—" He hesitated a moment, then shrugged. "Very nice."

Becca didn't move. She held her breath as her eyes locked with his. Reading the sincerity in his gaze, she smiled and gently resumed breathing. "Thank you."

Horses nickered softly, several heads lifted over the gates to observe the late visitors.

Josh turned and began to stride toward the far end of the barn as if he'd never spoken.

Becca followed, patting each horse as she passed by. When she and Josh drew near the end stall, a loud neigh pierced the quiet. Rampage thrust his head over the stall door and nodded, his ears pricked forward. Nostrils quivering, he whinnied again.

Beside her, Josh chuckled. She looked at him. He actually grinned at his horse. The expression softened his face, making him seem younger, much more approachable.

And infinitely, heart-stoppingly masculine.

"He's loud," she commented, stating the obvious.

Josh glanced down at her, his eyes lit in amusement. "Yeah, he does that every time I come near. I like it."

She nodded, smiling back. "I guess so. As greetings go, it's great. Have you had him long?"

"Several years." Josh rubbed the stallion's nose.

"Is that what you were doing at your ranch, raising horses, not cattle?"

Instantly the amusement vanished.

Becca regretted her words at the sudden change. She wished she could have caught them back when the hard, bitter look closed over Josh.

"No. The ranch ran cattle. I'd hoped to start a horse-breeding program. But I only acquired Rampage and Bonnie before the divorce, not much of a start."

She couldn't help herself. She reached out and touched his arm, her fingers registering the strength and heat of his muscles beneath his shirt sleeve. She gripped him tightly.

"I'm sorry. I didn't mean to bring up bad memories. You must have been devastated to lose your wife like that."

He cocked his eyebrow and turned to face her, lifting her hand from his arm and holding it. His palm pressed against hers. His fingers held her gently, as if he didn't realize he hadn't released her.

"Hold on a minute, Becca. Before your romantically inclined mind rushes off on some totally wrong track, let me tell you a bit about my marriage. Tiffany and I weren't in love. At least not with each other. I wanted a place of my own. She had a place she couldn't run. It was an agreement we made, marriage to give us what we both wanted. My mistake was in thinking it'd last forever."

Becca stared. He was talking more of a business arrangement than a marriage.

"You didn't love her?" she whispered, scandalized.

He shook his head, his eyes narrowing at her disapproving disbelief.

"I liked her, she liked me. We both had something the other wanted. The only mistake I made as I said was in thinking it'd last forever. And in not getting some of that ranch deeded over to me. It was in poor shape when we married. I worked hard, we both did, really, to get it going again. Once we were in the black, Tiff decided she'd had enough. She sold it, divorced me and left for New York."

"And you got nothing, after all your work?" she asked, secretly appalled at the tale.

"Some money, to compensate me for my time and effort." His tone was bitter, his voice scathing. "But money doesn't compensate for loving the land, for building something up, knowing your own work made it a success, then losing it without any say in the matter."

"I'm sorry," she said.

He shrugged, rubbing his thumb across the back of her hand absently. "Wasn't your fault."

"I'm sorry you lost your ranch."

"It never was my ranch. I lost sight of that. It's a mistake I won't repeat. I aim to buy one. When I have my name on the deed, then I'll know it's mine forever. Nothing and no one will be able to take it from me then."

"So you're saving to buy a ranch?"

Josh nodded, his eyes dropping to their linked hands as if seeing them for the first time. Slowly he released her fingers.

"I've got the money from the settlement plus most of what I earned this last year. I figure working a few months for you will give me the rest of what I need for a hefty down payment."

She turned away. Her brother would have had land deeded to him had he come home, and he didn't want it. Josh was a man who loved ranching, wanted a place of his own very badly, yet it might be a long time before he could afford it. Life wasn't very fair sometimes, she thought.

"So the next time you marry, you'll have the ranch in your name first," she said.

"I'm not looking to get married again," he replied.

"But not all women are like your ex-wife. You might find someone who you'll fall in love with and will want to get married to. What about children? Don't you want someone to leave that ranch you're talking about?"

He remained silent a moment. "I've knocked around a lot, Becca, haven't found this love you're talking about. Maybe one day I'll want kids. If so, I'll look for a wife. But not until I'm settled, not until I'm sure nothing can take away my land."

"You'd want it free and clear, in that case," she said.

"You're right."

She reached out to rub Rampage's soft nose. He blew against her palm and pushed into her hand. Becca turned to Josh. He stood much closer than she'd thought, almost touching her. The radiant heat from his body surrounded her. She again felt an overwhelming awareness of the man like nothing she'd felt before. She wanted him to take her hand again and hold on forever. She wondered what it would be like to have him pull her against his hard frame and hold her. Just hold her like no one had done in years.

Wondered what it would take from a woman to cause him to fall in love.

She must be losing her mind. What little she had left.

"You all right?" he asked, looking at her closely.

She nodded. "I need to get home."

"You want any of your horses bred?" he asked, as if to delay her departure.

"With Rampage?"

Josh nodded.

She shrugged. "What's the stud fee?"

"No charge."

At her look of surprise he looked at the horse.

He hadn't meant to say that. He charged a lot for stud services. Rampage was a proven sire, his offspring had his even temper, his stamina and his conformation.

But for some reason Josh wanted to give something to this woman. Perhaps because she'd looked so forlorn this morning after getting the letter from her brother.

Or maybe it was the way her sister seemed so unfeeling.

Becca was alone in holding on to her ranch. It seemed as if the others in her family did little to help.

And he didn't want to be one of the takers. He wanted to do something for her.

"You'll have to see my mares, first. Solid quarter horse stock, but nothing special," she said slowly.

"I'm not looking to breed a champion, but you can have him cover the mares if you want some more horses."

"Thank you, Josh. I'll let you know."

Confused by the offer, she needed time to think. Becca knew Josh could get top price for stud services. If he was so anxious to save up money enough to buy his ranch, why pass up an opportunity?

She didn't want to take advantage of him, yet the chance to get a couple of colts from such a fine stallion was tempting.

"In the morning, if you don't have other plans, I'd like you to ride out with me. I want to see the rest of the stock," Josh said.

"We can leave at first light as long as it isn't raining," Becca said, turning away from the stall.

"I'll be ready."

"Well, did your cowboy appreciate your getting all dolled up?" Suzanne greeted when Becca walked into the kitchen.

Her eyes flickered beyond Becca before settling on her face. "Didn't come back with you, did he?"

"I had dinner with the men. We discussed the spring sale. You could have joined us," Becca said evenly, ignoring her sister's dig.

"Oh, Becca, that's so boring. I'll be glad to leave the place."

"We need to discuss that, too, Suzanne, but not tonight. I've had too many shocks today. I'm not up to it."

Her sister studied her face. "You do look beat. Go to bed. I'm not leaving for a couple of weeks. Time enough for you to bring up all the reasons I should stay. But it won't do any good, Becca, I'm determined to leave on my birthday."

"You never mentioned it before," Becca said.

"I didn't know Marc was going to pull a trick like he did. I thought he'd be here to support me. The rat. I'd like to get my hands on him."

Since Suzanne expressed Becca's very thoughts, she

couldn't add anything. She nodded. "I'll see you in the morning."

She thought more about Marc while she got ready for bed, but time and time again her mind shifted to thoughts of Josh Randall. Climbing in the bed she'd had since she'd been a child, Becca wondered if she'd done the right thing in hiring the man.

That afternoon she'd called the references he'd given when he'd been out acquainting himself with the ranch, though Bob Mason's recommendation would have been enough.

She refused to admit she'd been curious to what his former bosses would say. Each one she'd talked to spoke highly of Josh. He knew the cattle business. He knew horses. He set high standards, then lived up to them. He was well liked and respected.

She had seen some of that at dinner. After only a few hours with the cowboys who worked the Lazy M, he was already afforded respect.

A man of few words, she remembered his comments about her hair. It looked pretty. You look very nice. Very nice. Not the most flattering of compliments, but such from Josh meant a lot.

Despite Suzanne's teasing, Becca was glad she'd dressed up a little, glad she'd worn her hair loose.

Glad Josh had tucked back that errant strand, letting his fingertips brush across her cheek. Smiling in memory, she turned on her pillow and promptly fell asleep.

"Oh, no," Becca moaned when she awoke. It was still dark, and from the sound of water in the downspout, it was raining. She was so tired of rain!

Slowly she rose and walked to the window. Drawing the curtain back, she saw the sheeting water on the glass. Shivering in the coolness of her room, she hurried to dress.

She fixed a quick cup of tea and stood by the kitchen window as she nibbled on a bagel. Lights shone from the barn; she saw men moving as silhouettes against the illumination. Everyone was getting ready for the day— grumbling good-naturedly about the rain no doubt, but no one would sit it out. Nothing would get done if they waited for dry weather.

Donning her long slicker, she slapped her hat on her braided hair and headed for the barn. Slithering and slipping in the thick mud, she arrived in the large building without mishap.

"Good morning." Josh came from the tack room, nodded when he saw her.

"Good morning. It's raining again," she said, then wanted to kick herself for stating the obvious.

Suzanne would never have said such a dumb thing.

He looked out at the steady downpour then glanced back at her. "Are you the wicked witch of the west? You'll melt in the rain?" he asked.

She smiled and shook her head at his reference to The Wizard of Oz. "No, I guess not."

"Then there's no problem. I've saddled your horse for you. Trent told me which one was your favorite."

She was touched. For as far back as she could remember, no one else had ever saddled her horse for her. Her dad wanted her to be self-sufficient. And once she habitually saddled the gelding, no one else thought to offer. Until now.

"Thanks, I could have managed."

"I'm sure, but it didn't take much. Come on, I'm ready to ride."

She waved to the other men starting the day's work. Trent forked clean hay into the stalls he'd already mucked out. Jason rode out of the barn, leading a pack horse piled high with fence posts and rolled wire. Two more cowboys followed him.

Becca took the reins and prepared to mount her old gelding. Before she knew it, strong hands encircled her waist and tossed her up into the saddle.

"I've been mounting horses since—" She glared down at Josh.

Josh slammed her boot into the stirrup. "Since you were two, probably. Most ranchers start their kids young." Tucking her slicker around her leg, he glanced up at her and smiled.

Becca's insides melted. She forgot every word she'd ever learned. The most delicious warmth invaded every cell in her body. She wanted to stare into Josh's dark blue eyes until time ended. She forgot where she was, what day it was, who milled around them.

There was only Josh and her alone in a hazy world of two.

"That should keep you dry for a while anyway. No way to stay completely dry in this downpour. The rain's good for the grass, though."

He moved around the horse and tucked the slicker around her other leg, his hand resting on her knee when he finished.

Becca tightened her leg against the saddle, trapping his fingers. Leaning over until the brim of her hat touched the brim of his, she met his gaze. "I've been taking care of myself for a long time, Josh Randall. I can mount my own horse and tuck in my own slicker."

He smiled again and the blue grew brighter in the eyes she gazed into. "I reckon you can, but it was my pleasure," he drawled.

She flushed, wanting to pull back, but determined to hold her own, she resisted. "Are you flirting with me, cowboy?"

His right hand trapped between her knee and her saddle, he raised his left hand and drew one finger along the side of her jaw.

"No, ma'am. Against my code of ethics to flirt with my boss. Unless she invites it, of course."

Becca caught her breath.

For one dazzling moment she was almost tempted to invite it. Instead, she snatched his tantalizing finger away from her face, her hand holding his as his fingers entwined with hers. She couldn't look away.

"I'm not."

Her voice came out weak, breathless. She wished she hadn't moved his hand. Wished his thumb had brushed over her lips. Involuntarily, her gaze dropped to his mouth. For a long moment she tried to envision what it would be like pressed against hers.

"Good thing—you'd be hard to resist."

"If I invited flirtation, why would you resist?"

She couldn't believe she was having this kind of conversation. She should have slapped away his help with the slicker, taken charge of the situation and insisted they head out to the herd.

Instead, she was mesmerized by his rumbling voice, his enticing words, his provocative touch.

"You're not the kind of woman for a lighthearted flirtation. You are a dyed-in-the-wool romantic if ever I saw one."

"I am not."

"Honey, anyone who'd look as horrified as you did last night when you found out I didn't marry Tiffany for love is one romantic lady."

She jerked her hand free, pushed his hand away from her knee and sat up. Resettling her hat firmly on her head, she reined the horse to the left and headed out of the warm, dry barn and into the cold rain.

She'd just made a fool of herself in front of her new foreman. She'd spent years trying to maintain control of her father's ranch, ignore the suggestions made by some of the more randy cowboys, fought long and hard to make it in a man's world, and then almost ruined everything because of a pair of dark blue eyes and a man's touch that set every nerve ending quivering.

It wasn't fair.

Josh caught up with her, Rampage moving docilely along in the rain.

"Show me the mixed herd. Then you and I are going to sit down and seriously figure out what you can expect at the sale and just how we are going to orchestrate that sale."

Becca set off at a fast pace. Interested in seeing for herself just how Josh operated, there was no better time. They rode far and wide on the sprawling range that belonged to the Lazy M. Josh questioned her about all aspects of the operation.

Thanks to her father's tutelage, Becca was knowledge-able. She had all the answers at her command and was pleased at the depth of knowledge Josh displayed.

At one point he reined in beneath a small stand of cottonwoods. The rain didn't penetrate beneath the leafy trees. Reaching into his saddlebags, Josh brought out two thermoses.

"Here. I want to take a break and warm up a bit. It's cold out here."

She reached for the thermos and unscrewed the top. The fragrance of hot chocolate filled her nostrils. Smiling, she poured some into the cup and sipped. It was warm and sweet and thick and very chocolaty. "This is wonderful."

He studied her as she drank. She looked like a kitten again, this time finishing a bowl of cream.

He shook his head. Was the rain causing a short circuit in his thinking? He had no business thinking about Becca at all, except as his boss. Yet he couldn't take his eyes off her as she sipped the sweet brew. He liked looking at her, even covered in a bright yellow slicker and wet Stetson.

He swallowed a mouthful of hot coffee and almost burned his tongue. Whoa! He needed to pay attention, not stare at his boss. Not remember how silky her hair had felt last night, nor how soft her skin had been this morning.

He'd seen her gaze drop to his mouth and known if they'd been alone, if the other men on the ranch hadn't still been in the barn, he'd have kissed her until she clung to him.

He could still see the questions in her eyes, the flickering acknowledgment of interest. He'd like to explore it fully, but something held him back.

She wasn't a cowboy's flirt. She'd take such attentions

seriously, more seriously than he'd ever mean them.

And he wouldn't do that to her. She was too much a lady for such treatment.

"Do I have a hot chocolate mustache?" Becca asked, aware of Josh's stare.

He shook his head, looking away. "No. You look as if you like hot chocolate."

"I do! Much better than coffee."

"I suspected you might have a sweet tooth after the seconds you took on dessert last night."

She laughed. "I do. I'd eat cake and pie all the time if it was the slightest bit nutritional. Is your thermos filled with coffee?"

He nodded.

Touched he'd gone to the trouble to provide her with the hot chocolate, Becca's smile faded. She grew more and more interested in this man. He was an enigma. One moment the rough cowboy, bitter at the trick fate had played. The next moment he was consideration personified. She felt so special when he did something like tuck in her slicker or bring her a drink that wasn't coffee. How had he guessed she'd appreciate it? She didn't understand him at all.

But maybe she'd try to over the next few months. Hadn't he said he'd be here until the end of September?

By the time they returned to the barn, Becca was soaked and cold. Working in the snow didn't bother her as much as working in rain. And they'd had more than their share this spring.

She dismounted and flipped up her stirrup, preparing to loosen the saddle. Josh came around and took the reins from her hand, leading the gelding beside his own stallion.

"Hey!" Becca said.

"Trent," Josh called.

"Yeah, boss?"

Boss?

Becca swung around. She'd been the boss since her father died. Now the men called Josh "boss"?

Of course, he was their boss, just as she was his.

It'd take a bit of getting use to.

"Would you take care of Becca's horse? She needs to get to a hot shower and into dry clothes."

"Wait a minute."

he stepped over to Josh.

"Sure thing, boss." Trent smiled at Becca and led the gelding down toward his stall.

"I hired you to run the ranch, not my life," she began, anger beginning to simmer at Josh's high-handed ways.

He grabbed her arm and drew her to the side, his horse between them and Trent.

"Do you argue at every turn, Miss Montgomery? You're the ranking person on this ranch, take advantage of it once in a while. You don't have to prove anything to anyone. If you're cold and wet, get warm and dry, darn it."

"I'm not proving anything. I've already done that. But it's my ranch and I'll have the final say in how things are done and I don't need any cowboy taking care of my horse, I can manage myself."

"You'll run yourself into an early grave. Cut yourself a little slack, Becca. It won't take Trent twenty minutes to dry and curry the horse. He's got barn duty today anyway, so he's here. You're tired, cold and cranky. Go get warm."

It was so tempting. She was cold. She was tired. And she

liked having someone thinking about her for a change. The weight of the ranch was heavy. The responsibility enormous. For a second she welcomed sharing that burden.

"You hired me as foreman, let me do my job, Becca. I know what the men can do and where to draw the line. You can ease up somewhat. I can do the job."

"I know."

And she did. But for so long she'd been in total charge. It was awkward turning anything over to another person.

"Go get warm, Becca. You're turning blue."

"What about you, aren't you cold, too?"

"Sure. When I take care of Rampage, I'll get a quick shower before coming up to discuss the sale."

There was no reason to stay. She should turn and leave immediately. But still she hesitated, her eyes searching his. His hand held her arm, the horse enclosed them in on one side, the wall of the barn on the other. Still Becca hesitated.

"Want to come for lunch?" she said, drawing out the moment.

"Yes."

His eyes studied hers. Did he see something there? Was she offering the invitation he'd mentioned earlier? Was he strong enough to resist if she were?

She reached up and brushed his cheek. Flushing slightly, she held her fingertips up for his regard.

"You had a trail of water," she explained.

"I've got a trail of water all over. Want to wipe the rest away?"

His voice dropped in tone, his Western drawl became more pronounced as devilish lights danced in his eyes. Taking a step closer, he crowded against her, forcing her back against the rough wooden wall.

How far could he push her before she broke and ran for her life? he wondered. Slowly he moved his hand from her arm to her throat, his thumb brushing against the rapid pulse. She was cool to the touch, heating as his hand rested against her damp skin. Her eyes never left his, though her hand lightly clasped his wrist.

"Is this an invitation?" he asked softly, his eyes now firmly on her lips. He could almost taste her. How sweet would she be?

"Is this your idea of resistance?" she whispered.

"I lied."

"I'm glad." She closed her eyes and offered her mouth.

Josh was no saint. Without another word he closed his lips over hers and kissed her long and hard.

Four

Rampage bumped Josh and broke them apart. Josh pushed back against the horse, his eyes never leaving Becca. She licked her lips and looked everywhere but at the man who had just kissed her.

"I have to go," she said, sliding along the wall until she moved well away from the strong, silent figure who stood with his feet braced, watching her.

"It was only a kiss, Becca," he said softly. "Don't go running scared."

"I know what it was. And I'm not running anywhere. I'm going in to shower and change my clothes and eat. We can discuss the sale after lunch. Around one-thirty?" she asked, ruthlessly rescinding her invitation to lunch.

She walked steadily toward the open door and the rain that beckoned. She needed the jolt of reality the rain provided.

Josh Randall could kiss like no one she'd ever known. She'd never reacted to a kiss like that. And it scared her all the way down to her toes. He was all male and obviously expected her to be all female in return.

If his horse hadn't interrupted, she didn't know how long she'd have stayed pressed up against him, reveling in his touch, the taste of his mouth against hers.

Daringly she licked her lips once again, still tasting him. Her heart skidded then pounded. Raising her fingers, she tried to cool the heat in her cheeks. She knew she probably looked beet red.

Until she got herself under control, she wasn't going inside to let Suzanne see her. Once her heart stopped pounding, she'd be fine. Once she could collect her thoughts, she could go on. But until then, emotions flared and desire raged. For one moment, she almost turned around. But she kept walking steadily to the house.

Stalling until she was sure all traces of the kiss had faded, she entered the kitchen. She didn't wish to be teased. It had only been a kiss, as Josh had said. None of Suzanne's business.

Why was it that every second leading up to the kiss had seemed so natural that her every caution had been silenced?

Now she wondered if she'd made a mistake. She didn't flirt with the men who worked with her. She didn't want to be accused of giving off mixed signals. She treated them with respect and expected no less in return.

"You're back," Suzanne said when Becca entered the kitchen.

Suzanne wore dark long woolen slacks and a creamy sweater that clung to her like a second skin, rings sparkled on her fingers, silver dangled from her ears. She sat at the table frosting a cake.

"As you see," Becca said.

"And is our new foreman coming to lunch again today?" Suzanne asked, swinging around to stare at Becca.

"No."

At least she hoped he understood she didn't want him to come for lunch. She couldn't cope seeing him again that soon. She needed a little time to strengthen her defenses.

"He'll be along this afternoon to meet with me in the office. We need to discuss the roundup."

"It's late this year," Suzanne said.

"I know, but with the rains lasting so long there hasn't been a good time. Now I'm going to move ahead whether the rain stops or not."

"So that means we'll have tons of people traipsing through the house. Mountains of sandwiches and gallons of coffee to prepare," Suzanne grumbled, turning back to the cake she was frosting.

"And help from others to get the job done. You don't have to do anything you don't want," Becca said, staring at Suzanne.

Was she serious about leaving? Or was it just some sort of bid for acknowledgment that she was an adult?

"You know, you could have gone to college like Marc. "

"I don't want to go to college. It was all I could do to get through high school. What a drag."

"And what do you think you'll do if you leave here?" Becca asked, curious since Suzanne never mentioned leaving before.

She had things to tell her stepsister, but wanted to learn more about her plans first. Somehow she'd never expected either of her siblings to leave. She thought they loved the ranch as much as she did.

"When, Becca, not if. And if Marc's letter is any indication, there are plenty of job opportunities in California. Maybe I'll bum around L.A. for a while, stay with him. I'm sure to find something."

"Won't you miss the ranch?"

"Would you? Honestly, Becca. I remember how unhappy you were when you first came home after your father died. You loved college. You loved being on your own. Seeing more of the world than this poky town. I think that's more the reason Marc went than anything. You pushed him because you couldn't imagine anyone not loving college. If things had been different, would have come back to the ranch after college? If Matt hadn't died. would you have come back here and worked so hard? Or would you have gotten a job in a city and lived a different life?"

Becca slowly shrugged her shoulders.

"I did love college. And I had such plans. Nobody expected Dad to die when he did. Things just didn't work out."

"Don't you ever want to cut loose and try something else?" Suzanne pushed. "Sell this place and see the world? We could make a fortune. Invest the money and not have to work ever."

Becca turned away lest her sister saw the longing in her eyes.

Of course she wanted to do something else. She wanted the chances Marc had, to study what she wanted, try a new field. Spread her wings in a new city, expand her horizons. Be given a chance to make a difference.

She yearned to see something beside the mountains and valleys of Wyoming. There was an entire world out there and so much to see she ached with disappointment that she was stuck at the Lazy M her whole life.

But there was no use crying over spilled milk, as her dad

had often said. Things were the way things were. Unless something changed drastically, they'd probably remain that way the rest of her life.

While she felt tied to the ranch, it was also her heritage, the beloved homeland of her father. She'd never give it up.

"No, Suzanne, I don't want to sell the ranch."

"Well, I want to do more," Suzanne continued. "And before I'm too old to enjoy myself."

"I think it'd be good for you to stay with Marc awhile," Becca said slowly.

Where else would her lovely sister stay? Once she found out there was no money, she'd have to seriously consider her options.

"What's for lunch?" Becca asked, wanting to postpone the confrontation that she knew was inevitable.

"Sandwiches. It's a dreary day. I think I'm going into town to have my nails done. It's boring here and I need a change of scenery," Suzanne said, pulling open the refrigerator door. "I bet I'll never get bored in Los Angeles."

The house was silent when Becca finished her lunch. Silent and lonely. Suzanne had already left, saying she'd grab a bite to eat in town.

The rain had let up, though the sky remained overcast. Becca washed her plate and wondered how she'd manage when Suzanne left. She'd never lived entirely alone before.

She could eat with the men, that'd take care of that domestic aspect. It shouldn't be hard to find time to do the rest of the chores around the house, especially if Josh stayed to ramrod the place. Would he really have enough money by September to quit and buy a ranch?

If so, she'd better act while she had the chance. Maybe

she could take a short trip or two. Depending on how well the sale did, of course.

When she wandered into the office, Becca ignored the work piled on the desk. Instead she went to the small file cabinet near the window and opened the drawer that held all her travel brochures and pamphlets. She'd been collecting them for years. Planning where she'd go if she ever got the chance. Comparing different locations, different sights, she had planned fantasy itineraries to the tiniest detail.

She pulled out the folder for Washington, D.C., showing the monuments and parks, the museums and government buildings. Maybe she'd go there. See the White House, go to the top of the Washington Monument and get an aerial view of the city. She could sit in on the Congress, visit her representative.

She put the pamphlets back in that folder and reached for another. Maybe Key West. She'd love to see the ocean, to swim in it. Taste salt water instead of fresh. The writers made the locale seem so exotic, so wonderful. Would the air really feel soft against her cheeks? Would the sun—

"Ready?" Josh stood in the doorway.

Becca swung around, dropping the brochure. "I didn't hear you come in. Yes, I'm ready." When she leaned over to pick up the picture-perfect flier, Josh beat her to it. He studied the picture before handing it back to her.

"Ever been to Key West?" he asked.

"No. Have you?"

He shook his head. "Been to California, though, to the beaches in the southern part of the state. They're nice."

"I'd love to see the ocean. Doesn't much matter which one, just an ocean. Maybe I'll visit Marc and see the Pacific."

If he invited her to visit, and if she could get over being so hurt and angry with him.

"I like it here," Josh said.

"I don't have anything to compare it with. I want to travel and see some more of the world. I had such plans before my dad died."

Now she sounded like Suzanne. She could sympathize better with her sister if she wasn't so hurt that she wanted to leave.

"Like what?" he asked, watching her closely as if her answer mattered to him.

"I was in college when he died. I had to give it up to come home and run this place. I always wished I could have at least finished and gotten a degree."

"What were you studying?"

She wrinkled her nose. "I planned to study business administration, like Marc ended up doing. I hadn't even finished taking the required basics like English and history when I had to come back."

"You could still go to college."

"Maybe."

She dare not even think about her plans to take a few courses once Marc took some of the burden from her. It hurt too much to realize he'd never intended to help her on the ranch. Another postponement and she'd be too old to go to school.

She walked around and sat behind the desk. "Have a seat. You've seen the cattle, what do you think our prospects are for the roundup and sale?"

She felt safer with the width of the desk between them. And she made a conscious effort to keep her eyes on his, much as she longed to glance just for an instant at the firm lips that had moved over hers such a short time ago.

Much as she wished she could flirt like Suzanne and take that kiss in stride, she knew she could not. She'd like to say something personal, but business took precedence. And she felt more comfortable that way.

Josh dropped his hat on the corner of the desk and sat in the straight-back chair across from her, tilting back, his long legs stretched out, his thumbs tucked behind his belt buckle.

"I'd say you've got the basis for a good sale. If we muster the steers closer to the house, truck out from here, you can get it all done in a few days. Have you already had the buyers examine the herds?"

"Sam Stuart usually buys what I sell. He doesn't need to see anything ahead of time."

Josh frowned and brought the chair down on all four legs. "What do you mean?"

"He just buys what I cut from the herd."

She looked up from the notebook she'd pulled out to jot down everything they had to do.

"Becca, are you telling me for the last however many years you've just called up this Sam Stuart and told him you were shipping him cattle, and took whatever he paid you?"

"My father dealt with Sam," she defended. "I figured if he was good enough for my dad, he's good enough for me."

Josh closed his eyes briefly, then snapped them open. "It doesn't hurt to run some comparisons. It makes good business sense to shake things up once in a while."

"Like?"

"Like we'll call some of the brokers from different areas,

have them come and see the cattle, then make a bid on how many they'll buy and what price they'll offer."

"Auction the cattle?"

She'd never thought of that. Had no idea how to go about doing it.

"Shall I set it up?" he asked.

She nodded. "I'm wondering what other things I've missed," she said slowly.

"Not much, if what I've seen so far is any indication."

"But if I have, you'll let me know?"

"You can bet on it."

"Do it."

She reached for her map and spread it out on the desk. Soon she and Josh began to discuss the logistics of the roundup.

Twice his fingers brushed against hers as they pointed out different spots on the map to watch for problems.

Becca caught her breath each time, hoping she appeared cool and collected and that he couldn't detect the fluttering of her heart. Her hand tingled, her attention was more on the man studying the map than the plans discussed.

"That's it, then," she said, carefully moving out of range.

"How much did you make on the previous sales?" he asked, tilting back in his chair.

When she told him how many head she sold and the going rates, his lips tightened.

"I predict you're going to see an increase this year."

"I hadn't heard the price of cattle had risen drastically," she murmured.

She was tired of talking about cattle.

She wanted to learn more about Josh Randall. She could

ask him to dinner again. With Suzanne there, the conversation wouldn't remain centered on the ranch, her stepsister would see to that. Then maybe she could find out more about Josh.

Suzanne wouldn't hesitate to ask anything she wanted to know.

"It hasn't."

"You think I've been taken the last few years by Stuart, don't you?"

Suddenly she realized where he was leading.

"I didn't say that. I think this year will be better, that's all. We'll know more after the brokers come."

She nodded. "But you think we'll do better."

He nodded, his eyes on her.

"If I do get a better price, I'd share a portion with you," she said spontaneously.

Without this bidding process, she knew exactly what she could count on from Sam Stuart. He'd paid the same amount over the last three years.

Josh's expression hardened. "Not necessary," he stated flatly.

"I wouldn't be getting a different price if we didn't follow your suggestion."

"Just good ranch management."

"Well maybe sharing any increase with you would make it easier for me to accept use of your stallion as stud," she countered, irritation rising.

She was trying to do a nice thing. He didn't have to resist.

"I already said you could use Rampage."

His own expression was growing dark.

Tilting her chin, her eyes blazed into his. "I don't want

to be beholden to anyone. Rampage is an excellent horse. I'd be a fool to forgo any chance to have some of his get. But I'm not into charity, Josh Randall."

He leaned his forearms on the edge of her desk and nailed her with his angry gaze.

"And I'm not offering any, Ms. Montgomery. I needed a job, you gave me one, at a handsome salary. I'd offer Rampage's services to anyone I worked for."

She blinked, scooting back just a tad. "You would?"

The anger abruptly vanished.

"Yes."

"Thank you," she said primly.

He nodded and stared at her for another moment. Becca felt her cheeks warm. Despite her best intentions, her gaze dropped to his lips. She could still feel the delicious emotions his earlier kiss engendered.

Looking back into his eyes, she saw his awareness.

"If it turns out to be a very good year, you can take that trip to Key West," Josh said, flicking the corner of the brochure.

Becca nodded. Did dreams ever come true?

"Maybe. But that's a big if—and there's a lot of work to be done in the meantime."

"Nothing out of the ordinary. The rain makes it messy, but you've got a good crew."

"Where was your ranch?" she asked.

There were some things she couldn't resist knowing.

"South of here in Colorado."

"So you had the same weather pattern we have."

"Pretty much. The rain's late this year. Makes the range sloppy, but we can still manage."

He rose.

She watched him stand up. He was so tall he seemed to tower over her. She jumped to her feet to shorten the distance between them.

"You know a lot about cattle, why don't you want another cattle ranch?" she asked, prolonging the moment.

She didn't want him to leave. She liked being around him. A certain electricity sparkled in the air when Josh was near. A certain quickening in her senses—everything seemed sharper, more colorful, more in focus. She felt vibrantly alive.

"I like horses. And you have to admit I wouldn't have the problem of worrying about roundup in the rain."

She nodded, grinning up at him. "I reckon that's right. But are you planning to train them or just raise them for sale?"

He rubbed his chin in thought for a moment. Leaning against her desk, he cocked his head.

"For starters I want to train them as well as raise them. Maybe get someone else to help me. I'd like to provide some fine cutting stock."

She stepped around the side of her desk until she stood close enough she could reach out and touch him. "Good cutting stock's worth a lot of money."

"Yes. But there's more to it than just the money. I like working with horses."

"The start-up costs would be high. And it might be a while before you'd have any colts to train."

"I've figured it all out, Becca. It will take a few years, but I plan to do it right. As soon as I have enough money to buy a place, I'll start in breeding, work at something else to pay the bills until the first horses are ready to sell."

She watched him talk. His face grew animated as he told her some of his plans. It was obvious he wanted that dream in the worst way. Almost envious, she watched as he explained each stage, from the first moment he acquired his own land, to the champion horses he wanted to show. He had his dream and one day he'd realize it.

She had hers—but it looked more and more like she'd never attain it.

"How about your family? Can they help?" she asked at one point.

"I don't have any family."

"Oh." What happened to them? Why was he alone? She at least had Marc and Suzanne. And Eileen if she became desperate enough to count her stepmother as family.

He looked down into her silvery eyes and saw compassion. He didn't need it. He'd been on his own for a long time. True, he still missed his mother. His father had died when he was a baby and he'd never known the man. But his mother had been special. He still couldn't believe she had died so long ago.

For a moment he wondered what she would have thought of Becca Montgomery.

Something stirred within him. He reached out and brushed his fingers along her jaw.

"No need to look so sad, Becca. My folks died a long time ago."

"So you've been on your own for years, except for your wife."

He drew his hand back and frowned. "Ex-wife."

"Everyone needs someone on their side, Josh," she said softly.

For one stunning moment she wanted to be the one at his side.

"I've done all right on my own. I can make it."

"But who do you share the good times with?" she persisted.

His touch on her jaw had sent shimmers of anticipation through her. Would he kiss her again?

"With whoever is around me at the time. And lately there haven't been so many good times. But better times are coming."

"You married Tiffany to have someone to share your life with. When you get your own spread you might change your mind. You're not going to want to build something just for yourself."

"What is this, a psychological analysis?"

He didn't need her reminding him he was alone. Sometimes he got lonely. But usually he had enough work to do, enough plans to make. It kept the loneliness at bay.

"No. I'm curious about you, that's all," she admitted.

Her hands clenched at her sides to keep from reaching out to rub the line between his eyes, to ease the tension in his face. To touch him.

Josh straightened and reached for his hat. Looking down at her for a moment he was tempted to pull her into his arms and kiss her. Their earlier kiss had ended far too soon for him. But he didn't think Becca Montgomery was the love-them-and-leave-them kind of woman. And he vowed not to get tangled up permanently with a woman again.

At least not until he had his life the way he wanted it.

Becca owned a ranch that needed help. Tiffany had

owned a ranch that needed help. Becca was practically alone, would be once her stepsister left for California. Tiff had been alone, and so grateful for his help.

He refused to repeat the mistakes of his marriage. He'd learned from that experience and knew what he wanted in the future. While he might want to kiss this woman, and even make love to her, he knew he planned to ride out as soon as he had money enough to buy a place.

And when he rode out, he'd ride alone.

"There's nothing about me to whet your curiosity." He jammed the hat onto his head. "Nothing about me at all that you need to worry about. I'll let the men know the plans we've made. And I'll get right on calling those brokers."

He nodded once, avoiding her eyes, and left the room. His boots sounded loud in the afternoon silence as he strode through the kitchen. Closing the back door behind him, he scanned the sky. The rain had stopped and it finally looked as if the clouds were breaking up.

There was plenty of work to do and he'd get started immediately. The busier he became, the less time he'd have to think about Becca.

Though he couldn't help think about her offer to share a portion of the increase in sales. She needed a keeper. She had no business offering a stranger she'd just met a share of her profits.

Other men might take advantage of her. He'd watch out for her as long as he stayed. She saw everything through rosy glasses, though maybe this situation with her stepbrother and stepsister would change that. As far as he could tell, they'd taken advantage of Becca since her father died.

Not that it was any of his business, he thought, walking quickly through the muddy yard. He was here for business only. To earn enough money to buy his own place. Nothing else.

Five

There's nothing about me to whet your curiosity. The words echoed in Becca's mind. "You're wrong," she said softly as she listened to Josh stride away. "There's a lot about you that whets my curiosity and you have done nothing to answer my questions. You've only raised more."

One thing Becca learned over the last six years since her father's death was patience.

She'd waited patiently for Marc to finish college.

She'd patiently dealt with her stepmother when she dithered so much about what to do after Becca's father died. And again when she'd debated remarriage.

And she'd been more than patient with Suzanne's antics as a teenager.

She could afford to be patient a bit longer regarding Josh. He was staying for a while, long enough for her to feel confident she'd satisfy her curiosity.

Long enough for more heart-stopping kisses? The thought invaded her mind.

Unconsciously she licked her lips. She couldn't get tangled up with any old cowboy who passed through. But a mild flirtation wouldn't hurt, would it?

If she could pull it off, that is. She wasn't used to it. But she was a woman. One attracted to a sexy male. Surely some things were instinctive. She'd test the waters, make sure Josh knew she was interested. Let him take the initiative and see how far they went.

She frowned. Maybe he wouldn't take the initiative. So could she—without making a fool of herself if she misread the signs?

Mooning around like a star-struck teenager didn't get the work done. She turned back to the desk and began to post the invoices she'd received from the feed company. But it was harder to push all thoughts of Josh Randall from her mind.

By dinner, Josh had arranged for five brokers to visit the ranch over the next week. Becca called Sam Stuart and let him know how she planned to handle this year's spring sale. He didn't protest or try to talk her out of it, merely confirmed he'd be out within a day to check out her herd.

When she wandered down to the barn after dinner, it was to check on the horses, not because she hoped to run into Josh. At least, that's what she told herself. Disappointed to find no one in the barn, she turned without thought and headed for the bunkhouse.

When she opened the door, the warmth of the large living room enveloped her. One glance was all it took to see that Josh sat at the table to the left, playing poker with five of the other cowboys. The remainder were lounging in front of the television.

"Need something?" Josh asked when she closed the door.

"No. Just wanted to let you know Sam Stuart will be here tomorrow to check out the herd," she said as she wandered to the table and idly glanced around.

"Good. Jed Marshall and Bill Turner are coming tomorrow, too. You show Sam around, I'll take care of the others."

She nodded.

"Want to be dealt in the next hand, Becca?" Trent asked, fanning his cards close to his chest.

"Sure."

She pulled a chair up to the table, squeezing in between Jason and Trent. She could watch Josh from this angle and took advantage of his concentration on the game to study him.

They were playing with pennies, nickels and dimes, so the stakes weren't steep. Yet Josh concentrated as if this were a high-stakes Las Vegas game.

His dark hair gleamed in the lamplight, the planes of his face partially shadowed. He looked up, catching her gaze. His look was as intent for her as it had been for the cards in his hand.

Becca didn't look away. Emotions churned and tumbled within and her fascination grew.

Becca watched Josh deal with the same insouciance he did everything. Calmly flipping the cards out onto the table, his eyes locked onto hers and held. She caught her breath, her heart fluttering again. Was she destined to feel this unsettled every time she saw him?

Winking, he murmured, "Five card draw, one-eyed jacks are wild. Ante up, boys and girls."

The men each tossed a nickel for the pot

"I didn't bring any money," Becca said suddenly.

She felt almost breathless from the look in Josh's eyes.

She didn't touch the cards before her. Maybe this wasn't such a good idea.

"I'll stake you," Josh said easily. In two seconds she had a small stack of coins in front of her.

"I'll pay you back out of my winnings," she said airily.

His eyes lit in amusement but he remained silent. Blue eyes locked with gray as they stared at each other over the scarred wooden table.

When one of the other players coughed, Becca dropped her gaze. With a quick scan at the other men at the table, she picked up her cards. She'd forgotten for a split second where she was, that others were present. She'd been caught up in the magic spell of Josh's gaze and everything else had taken a dim and distant second place.

Foolishness, she chided herself. Slowly she rearranged her cards, then peeped over the edges to study the dealer. Foolish or not, he intrigued her beyond anything she'd ever known. His expression never wavered. His eyes held mocking amusement as he responded to the bets made by the other men. When they'd flash at her, they held something more.

By the time the evening drew to a close, Becca knew Josh had the quintessential poker face. Whether he held a nothing hand or a royal flush, his expression never changed. He had no annoying habits or revealing gestures. He remained cool, calm and in control. Much as she'd seen him since they'd met.

She wished just once she could guess what he was thinking.

"You've wiped me out, Josh," Trent said good-naturedly, pushing back his chair and stretching. "I'm gonna hit the hay. See you in the morning. Becca." He nodded to her and left the room.

One by one the others made excuses and retired to their rooms until only Becca and Josh remained at the table.

"Want to play another hand?" he asked.

She glanced at the pitiful pile of coins remaining at her place, then looked at the huge stack before him.

Slowly she pushed her money over. "I think I still owe you fifty cents."

"I'll give you a chance to win it back."

"The way your luck's running tonight, you'd end up owning the Lazy M."

She raised her shoulders and rotated them to ease the strain of sitting so long at the table.

"It's getting late and we have a lot to do tomorrow. I had fun tonight," she said almost wistfully.

"Stopped work for once?" he asked, lazily shuffling the cards.

"Don't believe all Suzanne says. I don't work all the time," Becca said, mesmerized by the way his strong hands handled the cards so easily.

She watched as he cut, shuffled, stacked. Over and over. They were strong hands, ones that had easily lifted her to her horse. Yet they could be so gentle when brushing a strand of hair away from her face. Dependable hands, working hands, rough and calloused.

She wanted to reach out and stop the shuffling. Twine her fingers with his and feel that strength. She wanted to feel the tingling awareness that captivated her each time he touched her. Would she feel it tonight?

"Thanks for asking me to join in the game. I used to play

when my dad was alive. I don't think I've played once since he died."

"You don't play badly, for a girl."

She jerked her face up to meet his, frowning in mock anger at the dancing light in his eyes.

"I'll have you know I did better than Trent and Jason. You merely had a run of luck tonight. Wait till we have a rematch."

"Don't bet the ranch, honey. Your eyes give you away every time. When you hold a good hand, they sparkle and shine. When you're disappointed in the cards, they almost dim. Don't ever play high-stakes poker."

She blinked and stared at him. He'd called her honey.

"No one else ever said that."

"Maybe they weren't watching you as closely as I was."

He'd been watching her? A shiver of excitement raced down her back. "Maybe next time I'll sit beside you so you can't see me so well."

He considered her suggestion and nodded. "That'd be fine. I still think I could tell."

Becca stood up. "Thanks for the tip, I'll wear dark glasses."

He smiled at that and dropped the cards, rising beside the table. "Then your cards will be reflected in the lenses."

"Good grief, I can't win, can I?"

"You did all right tonight."

"Yeah, for a girl."

He smiled again. "You are a girl."

She moved around the table, as intent as a cat stalking a bird. "Let me tell you, Mr. Hotshot Cardsharp, I'm a woman. I passed my girlhood a long time ago."

"That I know."

He reached out and drew her into his arms, his mouth covering hers without further ado. His lips were warm and coaxing and before she knew what she was doing, Becca responded with a welcome that surprised her.

She forgot everything, the problems facing her, the lateness of the night, the fact that she was in the living room of the bunkhouse with seven cowboys just a hallway away. Emotions roiled within as Josh pressed her soft body against the length of his hard frame. Desire flared as his hands kneaded the back of her neck, traced the curve of her spine. Pleasure seeped into every cell as he deepened the kiss. Becca floated in blissful delight.

The closing of a door down the hall broke them apart. Josh gulped in air and glared down at her with his dark blue eyes. "You need to get home."

"Yes."

Reluctantly she withdrew her hands from around his shoulders. Slowly her fingertips lingered just a moment longer on the strength beneath the cotton shirt. The tingle had been there. She dropped her hands to her sides and stepped back. She really didn't want to end their embrace.

"I'll walk you to the house," Josh said, his voice gruff with emotion.

"I can manage."

She turned to walk swiftly across the large living room.

"No one ever said you couldn't," he murmured as he reached the door at the same time she did. He grabbed his hat from the rack on the wall and waited for her to precede him.

The ground squished beneath them, still laden with

moisture. The sky had cleared, stars shone with particular brilliance in the darkness with no moon to compete with.

Becca relished the faint light. She couldn't think and didn't want Josh seeing something in her expression she wasn't willing to share. His kiss had been wonderful, like the one in the barn. But she wasn't sure she was up to kisses at night then working together as if nothing happened come daylight.

"Don't brood, Becca. I find you attractive, you must find me attractive." His hand caught her arm and swung her around. "Don't you?"

She gazed up at him, seeing only a silhouette against the starry sky. At least he couldn't see any more of her than that.

"I think that's obvious," she said.

"It won't interfere with work."

"I know. I'd draw the line there," she acknowledged.

"With this mutual attraction, we could do things together for as long as I'm here. I'm glad you joined us at the poker table tonight."

For as long as I'm here. With a rush of surprise she realized she'd forgotten he was a temporary cowboy, hired out only long enough to earn enough money to buy his own place. She hadn't bought his services for life. She was only providing a job until it was time for him to move on.

And she needed to make sure her ranch came first. It was the only stable thing she had. Marc deserted her. Suzanne wanted to leave. Josh wouldn't stay. The ranch was the only constant she could count on.

"I had fun tonight but I'm not sure about spending a lot of time together. I'm not very good at flirting and playing the field. I tend to take things too seriously. I don't want to end up falling for you, Josh, and I'm afraid that could happen if we spend too much time together."

There, she'd said what she'd feared from the first.

Holding her breath, she realized she almost wished he would sweep her off her feet, pull her into his arms and say he'd never leave.

"You're too smart to go falling for me, Becca. You know I'm not the marrying kind, nor am I planning to stay here forever. As soon as I have enough money, I'm leaving. But knowing that ahead of time, you can make sure you don't build castles in the air."

"I know."

But she had never felt so strongly attracted to anyone. She wasn't sure she could keep her perspective with him. Another of his kisses and she'd be ready to offer—

"I wouldn't hurt you," he said, brushing back a tendril of hair. His hand brushed gently against her cheek as before. His voice drifted soft and seductive.

"You wouldn't mean to, anyway," she replied. "But I don't think it's wise. Soon you'll be moving on—"

"Not for a few months. If then. It takes a lot of money to buy a ranch."

"You want to purchase one outright?" she asked in disbelief.

"Not possible. I do want to own a place free and clear eventually. That means no one and nothing can take it away from me. Next time I call a place my own, it'll be all mine. Or to start with, mine and the bank's."

She turned toward the house, thinking about what he said. The light shone in the kitchen but she knew Suzanne had long gone to bed. She didn't know how much money he'd saved, but she did know even the down payment for a ranch large enough to support his plans would take a huge amount of money.

And he planned to stay on the Lazy M until the end of summer. How much had he already saved? Would a few month's work be enough to afford the down payment for his ranch?

Silently they approached the house.

"Good night," Becca said as she stepped on the first step.

Josh stopped her by taking her shoulders and gently turning her around. His lips brushed against hers briefly. "Good night. I'll see you in the morning." He spun around and walked back to the bunkhouse.

Becca stayed in the shadows and watched until she couldn't see him anymore. He wasn't for her. Even if he weren't leaving, he was dedicated to getting his own place. His dream was to establish a spread and live his life on it.

Her dreams were to travel and to go back to school. Maybe it was time she figured out how to obtain those dreams before she grew much older.

Slowly entering the house, Becca realized for the first time how much she resented Marc's cavalier treatment. She'd been counting on his returning to take over running the ranch. In the back of her mind she'd thought that when he returned, she could at least take some trips. She could leave the ranch in capable hands and take off for as long as she wanted to visit different places. And maybe one day soon she could have returned to college.

Turning off the light, she made her way to her room, angry anew at Marc. She'd have made him an equal partner in the Lazy M. The decision had not come easily, but Becca felt he deserved it.

"You never gave a thought about me, though, did you, Marc?" she whispered as she prepared for bed.

Maybe tomorrow she'd look at her pamphlets again. If she did better with the spring sale, as Josh predicted, if, then maybe she'd take a trip—while she had someone to run the Lazy M before he also took off.

Becca finished breakfast and sat sipping her second cup of tea the next morning when Josh entered the kitchen.

"Good morning," she said. "Want some coffee? The pot's almost full. Suzanne likes it, so I generally fix a pot when I get up. Mornings when I need a jump-start, I take a cup or two, but I prefer tea. I can fix you a cup of tea, if you'd like. Though I can't imagine you drinking tea."

He waited until she ran through the words. When she stopped, he shook his head.

"Don't go getting skittish on me, honey. We've shared a couple of kisses, Becca. Nothing more."

She nodded, her gaze dropping to the cup in her hand. Glad to be holding something, she racked her brain for something else to say, feeling like a total idiot.

Josh crossed the room and poured himself a cup of coffee. Sitting opposite her at the table, he placed his hat on the chair beside him.

"Where's Suzanne? I thought she cooked."

"She does dinners. Lunch if she's here. But she doesn't get up this early as a rule."

"What else does she do around here?"

"Keeps the house. She's only twenty."

"She'll be twenty-one in a couple of weeks. Do you think she'll really leave?"

Becca shrugged. "The other day was the first I heard about it. When she finds out how hard it is to make a living when you don't have any experience or much education, I think she might realize this place isn't so bad."

"What about her share of the ranch? You going to let her cash out?"

Becca looked at him. "There isn't any share. Dad left the place to me."

Josh nodded as if satisfied. "I suspected as much. And you've been carrying the others ever since."

"He left Eileen a portion and some money. She had me buy her out right away, took the money and went on with her life. She was only in her early forties."

"What are you going to do about Suzanne when she asks for money?"

"Tell her there isn't any," she said slowly. "She'll probably go through the roof, but it is what it is."

"What time is Stuart coming?" Josh asked, changing the subject.

"About nine, why?"

"I want to be there when he comes."

"I thought you were going to show your brokers around while I showed Sam around."

"I changed my mind after watching you last night."

Instantly Becca grew alert, defensive. "What does that mean?"

"I don't want you making some sort of deal with the guy because he's bought cattle in the past. And with your expressive eyes, you're bound to give away any advantage we might have."

"I resent that. I've been doing fine for years. I don't need you coming in here and telling me how to run this place."

"You hired me as foreman, I'm watching out for the Lazy M."

His easy tone contrasted directly to her angry one.

"I am the Lazy M!"

"Give me a chance to do my job, Becca. Especially if I'm to get a cut of any increase in the sales this year."

Money. Of course, she should have known instantly. He wanted as much money as quickly as possible.

"And you don't trust me to make the best deal?" she asked.

"I don't know this Sam Stuart. He could be a good old boy giving you top dollar because he liked your dad, or a shark taking advantage of a woman who doesn't have as much experience as she needs."

She opened her mouth to refute his words, then shut it abruptly.

Sam definitely resembled the shark. Had he taken advantage of her over the years?

Money or not, Josh was right. She hired him to ramrod the place. If she stopped him, she hindered his work.

Besides, she had to admit she was curious about the entire process. And the end result. Would she gain more from the sale this year than last?

"Very well," she conceded grudgingly.

"You can come, too, if you want."

"You bet your boots, cowboy. If this works, I want to know how to do it myself next year."

"Well, well, isn't this cozy?"

Suzanne paused in the doorway for maximum effect. She wore a pale blue satin robe. Sleek and long, it displayed her lovely figure to full advantage. She'd taken time to put on her makeup and comb her hair.

"Good morning, Suzanne," Josh said, running his eyes appreciatively over her.

"I didn't realize you were coming to breakfast or I would have been down earlier."

She almost purred. Walking to the table, she pulled out the chair next to Josh and smiled at him when she sat down.

"Have you eaten yet or can I fix you breakfast?" she asked.

"I ate with the men. Just going over a few things with Becca."

Suzanne frowned. "Work again. Honestly, watch yourself, Josh, that you don't end up like Becca, all work and no play. Want to take the day off and go into town with me?"

Josh smiled and shook his head. "I've only been on the job a couple of days. Cut me some slack, Suzanne. I need to impress the boss, you know. Besides, it's going to be busy around here for the next few weeks."

"The roundup and sale. I know," Suzanne said.

"Today we have a couple of brokers coming to check out the cattle and give bids."

Suzanne looked at Becca. "Aren't you just selling to Sam, like always? He was a friend of Matt's. I'm sure he'd give the best price."

Becca pushed back her chair and took her cup to the sink.

"I'm seeing what else is out there. If Sam's got the best

price, he can have the cattle. There's a lot to do over the next few weeks, as Josh said. Can you arrange with Betty Warner and Joyce Fuller to help with the food when the roundup begins? I'll call around today and see who can spare some men to help out."

Becca almost looked at Josh to see if that would fit with his plans. But she didn't. It was still her ranch and she controlled the reins.

"Oh, I meant to tell you last night, but you didn't come in until after I went to bed," Suzanne began.

"Tell me what?" Becca turned and leaned against the sink.

"Mrs. Brown from the church committee stopped me in town yesterday and asked if we could contribute to the annual bake sale. I said yes. I'm making a cake and I volunteered you for a few dozen cookies."

Becca groaned softly. "I don't have time to make cookies for the bake sale. You should have asked me first, Suzanne."

The younger woman looked put out. "I didn't think it was such a big deal. Just make a couple of batches one night. I'll take them in when I go."

"I don't have the time," Becca said.

"It's not like I said you'd make everything. Just a few dozen cookies."

"She said no," Josh said, reaching for his hat.

"What?" Suzanne swung her gaze to him.

"Your sister said no. If she doesn't have time to be baking for some event in town, you do it. You volunteered."

He stood and carried his cup to the sink, stopping beside Becca and looking down at her. She seemed dazed.

"Who gives you the right to speak for Becca?" Suzanne demanded.

He looked at Suzanne, his eyes hard. "I'm not speaking for her. Just reiterating what she told you."

Suzanne rose, scarlet flags dotted each cheek. "Becca, rein in this cowboy before I get angry."

Becca looked at Suzanne and for the first time in years felt a bit of the weight of responsibility ease.

"Josh's right, Suzanne, I'm saying no. I will not bake the cookies."

"But I told Mrs. Brown you would."

"Then you either have to tell her I won't or bake them yourself. I've got more important things to do."

"But you always bake for this fund-raiser."

"I have in years past, and I would now, except the spring roundup is late and I'm needed elsewhere. Next time check with me before volunteering my services."

"There won't be a next time. In two more weeks I'm gone!"

Suzanne turned and flounced out of the kitchen.

Becca stared after her in dismay. She needed to tell Suzanne soon that there was no money coming from the Lazy M when she left. But first, there was Josh.

"Thanks," she said, raising her gaze to his chin, afraid to look into his eyes. "I haven't had anyone take my side in anything for a long time."

"No problem. She just got the bit between the teeth. I don't think she meant anything by it."

She wouldn't let herself mind that he defended Suzanne. She would have done so herself. But somehow she'd thought he'd stay firmly on her side. It sounded almost as if he were indulgent of her younger sister. Sighing, she turned away.

Suzanne was beautiful. Becca tried not to resent the fact, but sometimes it was hard to forget.

"I'll call around to line up help for the mustering," she said, heading for the office.

Josh watched her leave the kitchen. He wanted to go with her. She seemed so slight for the weight of all the responsibility that rested on her shoulders.

And she'd seemed grateful for his support against her stepsister.

Knowing what he did about the setup on the ranch, he suspected she hadn't had anyone champion her side of arguments in a long time.

Readjusting his hat, he pushed through the back door and headed for the barn. If he knew anything about human nature, there'd be tantrum to end all tantrums when Suzanne found out there was no chunk of change coming her way when she left.

Becca definitely would need support then, too.

He wondered if she'd let him be there when she told Suzanne or if she'd insist it was a family matter and exclude him. It'd be up to him to insist. After all, she'd tacitly agreed to place the ranch in his hands. He'd look after her as he did the rest of the place.

Even if it meant protecting her from Suzanne's temper tantrum.

Six

Cutting through the kitchen sometime later, Becca found Suzanne leaning against the counter, gazing out the window. She turned when she heard Becca.

"Hurrying after your foreman?" she asked.

Becca stopped and looked at her warily.

"The buyers will be here soon. I'm going out to meet them. I may be gone the rest of the morning."

"Watch yourself around Josh Randall," Suzanne said, her eyes narrowed as she studied Becca.

"What do you mean?"

"I'd suspect his motives, if I were you."

"Motives?"

"Sure. Defending the helpless maiden to get into her good graces. Let's face it, Becca, you're not exactly the type men fall over themselves for. Yet here's this big macho cowboy telling everyone what you will and will not do. For the good of the ranch? Or for the good of Josh Randall?"

"I hired him to manage the ranch," Becca said evenly.

"Sure, but why manage something if you can get ownership interest. Watch yourself, Becca."

Becca frowned and continued out to the back porch. Pulling on her jacket, she tried to ignore Suzanne's words.

Slamming her hat onto her head, she stormed off to the barn. She refused to let Suzanne's suggestions take root.

Stung by her sister's words about her appearance, she had to agree, nonetheless, with the sentiment. Men usually didn't even notice her if Suzanne was around.

But her sister was wrong. Josh didn't want part ownership of the Lazy M. He wanted a place of his own. She'd bet the ranch on it.

Smiling at the old saying, she spotted the men standing beside two saddled horses. Only last night Josh had warned her not to bet the ranch. She'd show him she could be difficult to read. Veering to intercept the men, she pushed Suzanne's insinuations to the back of her mind. She had business to attend to.

But the niggling doubt began. And throughout the day it rose to plague her.

Becca couldn't halt the warmth that ran through her as she spotted Josh. She picked up her pace to hurry over to where he stood talking with a short man wearing a white Stetson.

"Becca, I'd like you to meet Bill Turner. Bill, this is Becca Montgomery, owner of the Lazy M."

"Howdy, young lady. Pleased to meet you. Been talking with Josh here about your spread. Pretty grazing land. Bet you raise heavyweight stock."

"Yes, we do, actually. Do you buy much cattle from the Wind River area?" she asked, standing beside Josh.

Bill Turner was pretty heavy stock himself. She cast a nervous glance to the horses, hoping they'd be up to carrying his weight.

"Have in years past. Paul Robinson north of here sold

to me several years running. Then that dad-blasted Blake Hornblower trumped my aces more times than I care to remember. You asked him here to see the cattle?"

He looked sharply at Josh.

"No, but it might not be a bad idea."

"Stay away from him and I'll raise my ante another percent."

Becca looked at Josh, his gaze was as impassive as when he played poker.

"We'll just see what you ante up to begin with, Bill. You know I've got several other brokers coming to look at the cattle and give us a bid," he said quietly.

"Sure you do, boy. Did the same at your place a couple years back as I recollect. But we still managed to put together a couple of fine deals."

"We did, Bill. And had a few celebratory drinks, as I recall."

"Now, no need raking that up. My head hurt for two days. I don't think you ever blinked."

Josh allowed a slow smile, winked at Becca and shook his head. "I'm not telling. You ready to ride?"

"Sure am. Glad the rain stopped. Always hate riding around in the rain. Don't know why you folks persist in ranching. Can't stay inside in the rain like sensible folks."

"Or the snow," Becca said, deciding she liked the roguish old man.

And she was charmed at the glimpse of his relationship with Josh.

She smiled at Bill Turner. "I'll be glad to show you around the ranch."

"Now don't you try sweet-talking me into raising my bid.

I've got my reputation to consider," he grumbled good-naturedly as he mounted the horse Josh held for him.

"Becca knows more about this place than anyone. She can tell you all you need to know about the cattle. Just don't talk any numbers. I'm the one you deal with for that," Josh admonished.

"Sure, sure, boy. She softens me up and you come in for the kill."

Becca smiled at his nonsense and they set off. She glanced back once to find Josh's eyes still on her. She waved and settled around to face the front.

She liked Bill Turner. He talked the entire time they rode, telling her funny stories, usually on him. He never spoke down about another soul. But he did his fair share of pumping her for information, and she did her share trying to find out more about Josh Randall.

Had it been left to Becca, she probably would have sold the cattle to Bill based on her enjoyment of the morning.

Sam Stuart usually talked down to her. She'd accepted it. He'd done it when her father had been alive and she took no offense.

But after spending several hours with Bill Turner, hearing the respect behind his teasing banter, learning more about the business from his questions and explanations, she grew resentful that Sam had thought so little of her to treat her like a child.

She wondered how he fared with Josh. Her new foreman was too much the arrogant male to take any slights from Sam Stuart. She wished she could have been with the two of them. She would love to see Josh set Sam in his place.

But she wouldn't trade these hours with Bill Turner for

anything. She'd learned more about Josh Randall—how hard he'd worked on his place. How he'd turned it from a losing proposition to a showplace through hard work and determination.

And she'd picked up a bit of information about Tiffany, his ex-wife. She'd been tall and blond and demanding—just like Suzanne, she thought with a pang.

Was that why he was so tolerant of her sister? Because she reminded him of his wife? Ex-wife. Because he liked long-legged blondes with fashion flare?

"As I said earlier, missy, you've got a fine place here. With Josh running things for you, you'll soon have one of the best ranches around," Turner said as they rode back toward the barn.

"I hope so."

If Josh stayed long enough, she could take a trip or two as she'd long wanted. Get away from the ranch for a few months to see what the rest of the world held.

Sam and Josh were waiting in front of the barn for them when they rode in.

"Becca, nice to see you again." Sam tipped his hat, his eyes moving on to her companion when they dismounted.

"Sam Stuart, Bill. Turner. He's also looking over the cattle," Becca introduced.

"So I heard from your foreman. Turner." He held out his hand.

The formalities over, he turned back to Becca. "Why don't you and I walk a bit and discuss this, Becca?"

She glanced at Josh, but he gave nothing away, watching her steadily from beneath the brim of his hat.

"Sure."

She remembered Josh's admonition—do not negotiate.

After spending the morning with Bill Turner, she was more anxious than ever to work through this bidding process. It was fascinating, and she was learning so much.

"I don't mind telling you, Becca, I got the shock of my life when I arrived and that new foreman of yours said you were taking bids for the cattle this year. Shocked to the core," Stuart began as they walked away from the barn.

"Josh suggested it and I agreed with him. It makes sound business sense. I'm very interested to see how the process works."

"I've been buying cattle from the Lazy M since long before your father died. I bought from you over the last six years. And this year I let you delay the sale because of the inclement weather."

Becca looked sharply at him. Let her delay the sale?

"I don't see a problem, Sam. Check out the cattle. Make an offer. If it's the best, I'll sell to you. And if it's not the highest offer, then I'd be foolish to accept it if I could get more from someone else, wouldn't I?" she asked reasonably.

He frowned and turned, glaring back toward Josh.

"Just how much do you know about this foreman you hired? You better watch out that he doesn't steal you blind. The Lazy M's been a family operation for as long as I can remember. Family sticks together, strangers are usually out for their own gain."

Becca paused and waited, her gaze drawn to Josh. He was leaning against the corral fence, one heel hooked on the bottom rail, his leg bent casually. His hat was pushed back and he and Bill Turner were laughing at something.

She wistfully wished she'd stayed with them. Especially

since she didn't appreciate the lecture Sam was giving.

Family sticks together. Sam should have mentioned that to Marc and Suzanne. Josh had done more with the ranch over the last couple of days than Marc had done in the last four years. Josh was staying for a while. Marc didn't even plan to come home between graduation and starting his new job in California.

"If I had known you needed a foreman, that you were looking for one, I would have recommended a couple of men I know," Sam said heavily.

"It was a rather sudden decision. Marc's accepted a job in California. He won't be coming back to the ranch," she said.

Did that mean forever? she wondered suddenly. Would he still want to come for Christmas and other holidays? Or once in California, would he forget about the Lazy M and the years of his childhood spent here?

"What do you know about Josh Randall?" Sam asked.

Becca faced him. "Sam, I appreciate your concern. But this is my ranch and I'll run it as I see fit. Josh came highly recommended. I've liked what he's done so far, end of discussion."

She turned and began walking quickly back toward the corral.

Josh glanced up as Becca and Sam headed toward him. Something was wrong. Color rode high in her cheeks and even from the distance he could see the anger in her eyes. Swinging his gaze to the man beside her, Josh slowly smiled.

Obviously Sam Stuart had been less than tactful with his boss. She was flaming angry and he looked pole-axed. Probably didn't know what hit him.

"Problems?" he murmured as she drew even with him.

"Nothing I can't handle," she said.

Josh noticed her holding on to her composure and his lips twitched again. He suspected she'd like to knock Sam Stuart on his pompous rear.

"Josh'll be handling the bidding process. You need to deal with him, Sam."

Turning to Bill Turner, she smiled brightly and offered her hand. "It was a pleasure meeting you, Bill. If you convince Josh yours is the best deal, I'm sure we'll see a lot of you. Gentlemen."

Becca turned and headed for the house. When the door closed behind her, it released the men from the silence.

"Now see here, Randall, I've been dealing with the Lazy M for years. I don't know what you've promised Becca, but I won't see her cheated," Stuart said abruptly.

"Whee, boy, Stuart. I'd watch what I said around this cowboy. He don't take much guff and you're pushing the limit," Bill Turner said jovially. "Josh, my boy, do you want the bids in writing or will a verbal do?"

Josh leveled a narrow gaze on Stuart, his eyes dark. "I want the bids in writing this year. In the future, we might go to verbal, but for the first time, I want Becca to see exactly what the comparisons are. That way she can be sure she's not being cheated."

"My word's good enough," Stuart said in affront.

"So's mine, but if the boy wants it on paper, that's fine with me. I'll have it to you by tomorrow."

"There are three more brokers coming tomorrow. I'd really like to have all the bids in by the end of the week. We'll start mustering on Saturday."

Becca peeked out of the window. The men were still talking. Was she missing something? She like leaving the discussion with Josh. She realized how much easier things would be if someone shared the burdens of the ranch with her. As she had wanted Marc to do.

"Something going on?" Suzanne asked from the doorway.

Becca swung around, embarrassed to be caught. "No, I was just seeing if Sam left yet. Did you talk to Betty and Joyce about helping out in the kitchen?"

Suzanne nodded. "Everyone's delighted to rally 'round," she said sarcastically. "No wonder, it's about the only excitement they're going to find around here. Once the sale is over, I think I'll go into Cheyenne to get some clothes. I doubt they wear ranch attire in California."

"Suzanne—" Becca had to tell her about the ranch, about the nonexistent share her sister thought she had.

The phone rang. Suzanne reached for it and was soon animatedly discussing a dinner date. Becca knew the time had passed. But before the week was out, she needed to talk to her sister.

When Becca came into the kitchen for dinner, she noticed the third place set at the table. "Company?" she asked Suzanne.

"I invited Josh to join us." she said as she drew a roast from the oven.

"Why?"

Suzanne looked up, smiling slyly. "Just because you like to work all the time doesn't mean the rest of us do. I wanted a change of pace. And you've got to admit, he's easy on the eyes. Don't worry, once dinner's done, you can excuse yourself and go back to the office. I'll entertain Josh."

Becca bet she would. For a moment a shaft of disappointment pierced her. She wanted to be the one to entertain Josh. He'd said he'd like to spend time with her. She'd pushed him away.

Something Suzanne would never do. After her discussion that morning with Turner, she knew Suzanne probably appealed to Josh more with her blond looks than Becca ever would.

"Evening." Josh stood in the doorway, his hat held in one hand. He'd cleaned up and combed his hair. His white shirt contrasted with his tanned face. His jeans were new, dark, snug. Even his boots had been polished.

Becca's heart skipped a beat, then began to pound heavily in her chest. If she had known earlier that he was joining them, she'd have changed, washed her face and put on some mascara at least. She tried to smile, but her face felt as thick as molasses.

"Hello, Josh. Come on in, no need to stand on ceremony around here. I've put you here, beside me. Sit down. Can I get you some wine? A beer?"

Suzanne fluttered over to him, smiling up at him. Her blue silk blouse matched her eyes. The slim, cream-colored woolen pants displayed her long legs to full advantage.

"A beer would be fine," he said.

"Sit, I'll bring it. Dinner's ready. Your timing's perfect. Becca, can you get the salad from the refrigerator? I have everything ready."

Becca moved on automatic. She was fascinated by the display of charm, domesticity and flirtatiousness by her sister.

She ought to take lessons and learn something. A lot, actually.

"Did Sam Stuart call you after he left here?" Josh asked Becca as they began eating.

"No business at the table. You work during the day, but here we're relaxing and enjoying each other's company," Suzanne said sharply. "Tell us a bit more about yourself, Josh. What have you been doing all your life?"

Josh stared at her for a moment, then grinned.

"You're right. All work and no play-- All my life, huh? Ranching, mostly. Did some rodeoing to get some quick money."

"You must be good to make money at it. So many cowboys enter rodeo events, but there's only one winner."

"I did all right. It's a hard sport, though. Hard on the body."

"So you've traveled around the west, chasing the buckle?"

He shook his head. "No, Suzanne. I competed in some of the events in Wyoming and Colorado. But I never wanted to reach the national finals."

"I bet you could go to Las Vegas," she said, her eyes shining with desire for the bright lights.

"Been there."

He glanced at Becca. "You ever been to Las Vegas?" he asked, drawing her into the conversation.

She shook her head. "Denver's as far as I've made it from the ranch. I've never really thought about seeing Vegas."

"I know, you want Key West."

"Key West?" Suzanne asked, looking at Becca with

thinly disguised annoyance.

"I'd like to visit Key West," Becca replied quietly.

"You can visit Marc and me when we have a place at the beach in California," Suzanne offered generously.

"Have you talked to him about that?" Becca asked.

"No, but I will. Tell me what you liked best about the rodeo, Josh. I always go to the ones around here. I find them fascinating."

She found the cowboys fascinating, Becca thought uncharitably. Quietly she watched as Suzanne and Josh talked and laughed and made the most of the dinner time.

He hadn't laughed with her. He rarely glanced her way. She felt excluded and alone. Lonely.

Just as the meal ended, Josh turned the topic to the Lazy M and the coming muster. Suzanne gave in with good grace.

"If we're finished, why don't the two of you go into the office and have that discussion once and for all. I'll make some coffee and we can have it in the living room after you and Becca finish," she said.

Josh nodded. "Sounds like a plan. Becca?"

She rose and pushed in her chair. "Thanks for the dinner, Suzanne, it was delicious. We won't be long."

She led the way to the office, conscious of Josh following her just a step behind. She imagined she could feel the heat from his body surround her. She knew she could smell the scent of his aftershave. For some reason knowing he'd shaved before dinner bothered her. She didn't want to think of him becoming cozy with her sister.

"We could have waited until tomorrow, I guess," she said as she entered the office and walked slowly to the desk.

She'd much rather ignore work for a few hours. There

was so much more she wanted to know about Josh, so much more to discuss than the sale. She wished it was over and done with so they could move to the next step.

The next step in their relationship?

She caught her breath.

They didn't have a relationship. They had a business arrangement.

Right, that's why he'd kissed her—more than once.

Maybe she should have resisted. No, that would have been impossible. But she could keep her distance from now on.

Except they were alone in the office. They really didn't have to discuss the roundup, they could do that tomorrow when the next brokers visited.

"Josh."

She turned, and he was right there.

"Yes?" His hand came out to tilt up her chin. He stepped closer. "There's nothing to discuss, is there, Becca?"

She shook her head, feeling scorched by the touch of his fingers against her jaw.

"I'm flattered."

"Flattered?"

"That you cut me from the herd, so to speak. Getting us alone in here, away from Suzanne."

When he lowered his mouth to hers, she didn't move. She scarcely breathed. It was heaven. She wanted more kisses. She wasn't foolish enough to turn away. Suspecting she was becoming addicted to his touch, she moved closer, wanting more.

The shrill ring of the phone shattered the moment.

"Darn it." She stepped to the desk and snatched up the receiver. "Hello?"

"Becca, how's it going? This is Marc."

"I recognized your voice. Where are you?"

Josh stepped closer, watching the expressions chase across Becca's face.

She frowned. "It's Marc," she whispered.

"You got my letter?" her brother asked.

"Couldn't you have at least called? Why not come home and discuss it with me? That was pretty cold, Marc, to find out by a letter you weren't coming back."

"Yeah, well, I figured you'd try to talk me out of it and I didn't want the hassle."

Josh tipped the receiver slightly away from her ear so he could hear. His head came close to hers, his breath brushed across her cheek.

Becca forgot her anger at her brother. She became attuned to the man beside her. She wanted to slip the receiver back on the phone and turn to Josh. Have him gather her in his arms and tell her he'd shoulder some of the burdens that grew so heavy.

"I don't think you can blame me for being a bit surprised with the turn of events. I thought you were studying agriculture and agribusiness. Never once in the last four years did you mention you didn't want to return to the ranch," she snapped.

"Get off my back, Becca. I've accepted a position with a high-tech firm in the L.A. area and I'm heading that way tomorrow. We need to discuss if you want to buy me out of my shares in the ranch or if I should put them up for sale to the highest bidder."

Becca heard the hint of bravado in Marc's voice. But the effrontery of his challenge left her speechless. Had he owned part of the ranch, he'd have sold it to anyone who offered money?

This was her home, the ranch her father had built.

And Marc thought to sell out to the highest bidder?

"You have no share in the ranch," she said, cold with anger.

"What are you talking about? Matt left me a portion. He often said Suzanne and I were as important to him as you were. And Mom said Matt looked after us. Don't think you can keep my share without coughing up some money, sister dear. If I don't get it from you, I'll get it from someone else."

Becca's eyes met Josh's. She saw the anger in his. His hand covered the mouthpiece.

"Tell him to take it up with his mother. Let her explain why there's nothing for him from the Lazy M," he said softly.

Suzanne appeared in the doorway, carrying a tray with three coffee cups and a plate of shortbread cookies. She stopped suddenly when she saw Josh and Becca's heads together sharing the phone.

"Who is it?" she asked.

Josh straightened and stepped away from Becca.

"It's Marc. Want to speak to him?" Becca asked as Josh's hand fell away from the receiver.

Suzanne carefully put the tray on the corner of the desk.

"Becca, I'm warning you—" Marc's voice came over the line.

"Marc, I suggest you call your mother and talk to her about this. You and Suzanne were both under age when Dad

105

wrote his will. And when he died."

Her gaze snagged Suzanne's and held it. She'd tell them both at the same time. She should not have to tell either.

"My father left a portion of the ranch to his wife and the remainder to his daughter by his first marriage, me. Call your mother, Marc, ask her what happened to the share she inherited."

When he slammed down the phone she winced and held the receiver away from her ear. Slowly she replaced it.

Suzanne looked at her, calmly, almost serenely.

"Let me guess, then Marc can confirm it when I talk to him. Mother sold out when she left right after Matt died."

Becca nodded.

"We have nothing."

Becca stared at her. "You have a home here any time you want it," she said.

Color stained Suzanne's cheeks as her eyes narrowed.

"You paid for Marc's college. It wasn't from his share of the ranch, was it?"

"There are no shares. I'm the sole owner of the Lazy M," Becca said slowly. "But you and Marc are family. Dad would have paid for both of you to go to college, so I just did what he would have wanted."

"So I've been living on charity over the last six years," Suzanne said as if to herself.

"Hardly charity, Suzanne. You're my sister," Becca protested, reaching out to touch her shoulder.

Suzanne shrugged away Becca's hand.

"Stepsister, Becca. My mother married your father. But we aren't really related."

"You and Marc and Eileen are all the family I have," Becca protested.

"We're not related at all. And if there's no money for Marc, I'm sure there's none for me."

"Your mother has some responsibility here," Josh said.

Seven

Both women swung around to look at him. Becca forgot he was even in the room.

"I suggest you give her a call as Becca suggested. If there's any money to change hands, she's the one responsible, not Becca."

"This is a private matter between Becca and me," Suzanne said. "I suggest you leave."

"I'm concerned about the Lazy M and its boss."

"Watch yourself, Becca. Now that Josh knows you own the whole place, no telling what he might do to sweet-talk you into granting him a cushy job for life."

"Suzanne—"

"Not now. I'm going to call my mother."

She turned and stormed from the room. Becca could hear her footsteps as she headed toward her room. The slamming door caused her to jump.

"I should have told her before. I should have told them both before," she said forlornly.

"Their mother should have told them. And when she left the ranch she should have taken her children with her. You were too young to have such a responsibility."

Becca raised her chin. "They're family."

"A step family, honey. And if the indications I've seen since I've been here are an example, I'd say you're the only one caught up in the fantasy of close family ties. Suzanne and Marc both strike me as out for their own main chance."

"Suzanne's young and disappointed. I think she thought she was going to get a large amount of money."

"And Marc? What excuse are you going to make for him? He apparently lied to you for four years, led you on, kept you thinking—until he had his future set—that he planned to join you on the ranch. Then he kindly lets you know in a letter."

It was a harsh truth. But the truth nonetheless.

She turned away and walked to the window, gazing out over the hills. The wind rippled the grass until it looked as if it were moving in the twilight. The last rays of the sun glimmered over the mountain ridge. The sky was already growing darker.

Tears stung her eyes, but she blinked them away.

"They are family," she repeated softly, as if to herself. "If we make more in the sale as you suggested, I could give them each a nest egg."

"They're taking you for a ride, Becca. You have to decide. Do you want to be their banker, doling out money for the rest of your life, suspecting money is the only tie between you and them? Or will you stop bribing them and then find out if there's truly the family bond you think there is?"

He spoke harshly, but facts were facts. She was setting herself up for heartache if she thought she could make Marc and Suzanne cling for any reason beside money.

"If the ranch is all yours, I'd suggest holding on to it.

Don't let a soft heart run your business," he said.

She stared out into the darkening sky. Was owning a ranch more to him than family? Or was Suzanne's suggestion right. Did Josh want her to hold on to her ranch until he could get part of it? She closed her eyes in hurt, anger and confusion.

"And your own experiences make you an expert on family bonding, I suppose," she said scathingly.

"If you are referring to my marriage, it sure points out how families shouldn't be."

"I'm sorry, I shouldn't have said that," she said, leaning her head against the cool glass.

She looked young and vulnerable standing by the window, as if the weight of the world crushed down on her shoulders Josh thought as he stepped closer.

"You have it right, however. My relationship with Tiffany wasn't ideal. And she served me a bad turn by selling the ranch out from under me once we made it profitable. I never had a hint it was coming," he said, watching her.

"Like Marc's letter."

Josh rested his hands on her shoulders, gently massaging away some of the tension.

"Like Marc's letter," he agreed.

"So I'm all alone," she said sadly.

It twisted his gut to hear her sad words. He wished he could do something to change things, to make Marc and Suzanne want and need Becca as much as she wanted them.

He'd only known her for a few days. There was nothing he could do to shelter her from the harsh realities of life or the circumstances that were unfolding.

"You're hardly alone. You've got a loyal crew working

for you. Your sister would be leaving some day anyway, if she gets married. She'll come to visit. You'll get married yourself one day. Look on it as a part of growing up," he said, knowing the words were inadequate, but not coming up with anything better.

"Easy for you to say, you're already grown up."

She missed her father more than ever. Missed the carefree days of her childhood.

"And had some hard lessons to learn along the way," he concurred.

"I like the work you're doing here, Josh. You can stay as long as you like. Maybe even marry another rancher," she said lightly.

Maybe she should consider it, she wouldn't be alone anymore. He'd have his ranch and she'd have someone she could count on to stay.

His hands froze, dropped to his sides. "You'd be the last woman I'd make a play for. I married a rancher once, remember, it didn't work out."

"I'm not planning to build it up and then get rid of the ranch," she protested, turning around to face him, startled to see the harsh lines of his expression.

"What do you want, Becca? I thought you yearned to travel."

"I do. Some days I want to be as far from Wyoming as I can get. I want to see the world, walk down a street I've never seen before, hear accents totally foreign to a Western drawl."

"And I want a place of my own. I've knocked around for years. It's time I settled down and built something with my life. We don't want the same thing. And I refuse to let myself get emotionally tied again to some land that could be taken from me on someone else's whim."

"I'm not planning to sell the Lazy M!"

"If traveling is what you want badly enough, you could decide to sell the ranch one day—depends on how much you want to experience other places. You'll get a bundle, enough to stake you elsewhere. Fund a nomad life if that's what you chose."

She rubbed her forehead, the beginnings of a headache creeping toward the surface. "No, I can't do that. I won't do that. This is my home. It's all I have from my dad. I'll never sell it!"

She met his eyes. "But you're right, marriage between us would be foolish. You like tall blondes and I sure don't come close."

"Where did you hear that?" he asked, going very still.

"Bill Tucker told me about Tiffany."

"Out of the blue, he just volunteered information about my ex-wife?" Josh looked incredulous.

She swallowed nervously. "Not exactly. I asked about her."

He gripped her shoulders, his hands not soothing this time, but hard and harsh. "I resent your questioning him about my past!"

"Well, you never tell me anything. You talked more about yourself at dinner tonight than since I've met you. Doesn't take much to open up to Suzanne, does it? She's tall and blond and very pretty."

"And she asked questions. She wasn't afraid to show an interest."

"And you were sure quick to respond."

"If you want to know anything, you could ask," he said.

Tilting her chin, Becca met his gaze unflinchingly. "There's nothing more I need to know. Please let me go, now. I don't need—"

He cut her sentence short when he lowered his mouth to hers and kissed her. It took two seconds for Becca to close her eyes. Josh drew her up against him, reveling in the feel of her soft curves pressed against his harder muscles. Gathering her closer still, he deepened the kiss.

He didn't want to become entangled with the pretty owner of a ranch. There was no future in any relationship between them.

But for tonight he'd forget his goal. For tonight, she looked lost and forlorn and he wanted her to feel better in the worst way.

A click in the hallway broke his concentration. Slowly he raised his face, pleased to note Becca's breathing was as erratic as his own. Glancing over his shoulder, he saw nothing.

She pushed against him.

"Let me go," she whispered.

Opening his arms, he released her and stepped back. Glancing around the office, he remembered his hat was still in the kitchen.

"See you in the morning. We have three brokers coming tomorrow. You can ride out with one of them."

Becca drew in a breath to let him know she was perfectly capable of deciding what she would do regarding the brokers, but Josh had already spun around and left.

"Bossy," she muttered, listening to the sound of his footsteps until she knew he'd gone out the kitchen door.

Slowly she sank back onto the edge of the desk, her emotions in turmoil.

First the call from Marc, then the scene with Suzanne, then she had practically asked a cowboy she'd known only a few days to marry her.

She should be glad he turned her down. Maybe he wasn't kissing her to get her ranch. She shook her head. Clearly she needed to get some more rest. She'd think about her future later. There was the coming sale to get through first.

And Josh's kisses to ignore.

The last person he'd get involved with was her. Hadn't he said so? Brushing her fingertips lightly against her lips, she sighed. She was very much afraid she wanted more.

The next two days were hectic. In addition to the usual chores around the ranch, Becca spent long hours with the brokers. They rode out to examine the cattle and then discussed the logistics of the muster and shipping.

She asked questions of each of the men, learning more and more about the entire process. Sometimes she wondered why her father hadn't handled the sales in the same manner.

Twice she'd thrown a triumphant smile at Josh when she'd felt the giddy happiness of the work overwhelm her. He returned neither, his gaze as impassive as when he played poker.

Suzanne pouted.

She avoided Becca where possible and spoke to her briefly only when need demanded. She'd mentioned her mother explained how she'd sold her share, but that she'd send Suzanne some money to tide her over.

It wasn't what she wanted and she blamed Becca for not telling her sooner.

That she was also angry with her mother didn't make her any easier to be around.

Becca tried to tell herself she didn't care. That she should have expected the reactions from both Suzanne and Marc since they both had assumed they'd receive a share of the ranch. Suzanne would either get over her snit or leave.

Becca had enough on her plate that she almost didn't care what Suzanne did. The fragile bond between them had shattered and Becca didn't know if she would ever feel the same again.

Josh was clearly showing her there could be nothing between them. He acted as proper as any cowboy on the place. But after the kisses he'd given, she didn't think of him like any other cowboy.

Friday morning Becca started in on paperwork immediately after breakfast. There was more than usual since she'd been neglecting it for several weeks. She really didn't like that aspect of ranching as much as she enjoyed being outside. But it played an important part of running the business and she needed to catch up.

"Got a minute?" Josh asked from the doorway.

Becca looked up, her eyes tired and dry. "Sure, what's up?"

Motioning him to take a seat, she rubbed her lids. It was already late morning. Time had flown as she had balanced accounts and paid bills.

Josh tossed down a half dozen sheets of paper, sat in the chair and tipped it back on two legs, watching her with lazy interest. "We've got all the bids."

Eagerly Becca reached out and picked up the papers. Skimming across the first one, her eyes lit in surprise. She laid it aside as she perused the second. Soon she'd scanned each bid.

"Wow," she said, and looked up into Josh's blue eyes. "Josh, even if we don't sell as many head as planned, I'll make almost twice what I made last year."

He nodded once. "And if we sell as planned, you'll make a bundle."

"Most of the quotes are within a few cents of each other."

"That's right. Are you surprised?"

"A bit. And for so much. I didn't realize beef was selling so high this year."

She scanned the fan of sheets again, a smile as bright as sunshine on her face.

"Sam's the lowest," she murmured.

Josh remained silent.

"Bill Turner's the second highest. I liked him better than that Jonas Sikes. Can we go with Bill?"

Josh shrugged. "It's your spread. You choose."

She looked at the bids one more time, then picked up Bill Turner's letter. "I choose Bill. What's the next step?"

She felt almost giddy with excitement. She wouldn't have money worries over the next few months with the amount gained from this sale. Even allowing for the percentage she planned to give Josh, she'd realize far more than any other sale since her father died.

More than enough for a trip or two. The thought came unbidden.

"We contact them all and let them know who we chose.

Then bright and early tomorrow, we start bringing the cattle in," Josh said.

"I want to call Bill."

He gave her a slow smile. "And you want me to call the others?" he guessed.

Nodding guiltily, Becca almost said she'd do it. But she didn't want to. And she had hired Josh as foreman. Other foremen did the dirty work, he could, too.

"Do you mind?" she asked uncertainly.

He chuckled. "Honey, you'll never make a tough boss if you feel bad about giving out assignments. It's part of the job and I don't mind a bit."

At the sight of his smile, heat spread through her. For a moment she didn't think about the ranch, or the sale they had to prepare for. She remembered only his kiss last night.

And he still called her honey.

Cowboys were notorious for loving and leaving. He might want some affectionate times with her, but he'd never lied or offered anything beyond what they'd discussed that first day.

And she wasn't up to risking her heart on some feckless cowboy who would be leaving one day soon. She'd do better to keep her distance.

"Tomorrow's Saturday," she said, pushing the memory back. "That means working on the weekend. The men aren't going to be thrilled with that."

"They'll do it. You might want to give them each a small bonus when the sale's complete. You'll be able to afford it from the proceeds. Then they can all have another weekend off. In fact, you'll need a weekend off, as well. We could drive into Cheyenne."

"No, I don't think so. I have too much to do around here."

The refusal came immediately, instinctively. The words were out before she could even think. She'd never gone anywhere with a man for the weekend. She couldn't risk it with Josh. She needed to keep on a strictly business footing before she found herself in over her head.

He shrugged. "Suit yourself."

He brought down the chair and reached for the letters still on the desk.

"I'll call the brokers, then get the men ready for tomorrow. The weather's supposed to be dry for the foreseeable future, so we'll bring the cattle in and hold them in that valley just over the hill from the barn. Tell Bill to have the trucks here Monday morning, early. We should be finished by noon Wednesday if things go well."

"Josh, I thought I heard your voice."

Suzanne entered the office, her eyes on the tall cowboy, ignoring Becca.

"Suzanne. How are you?"

Josh rose and smiled at the young woman.

"Great. I heard you from the hallway. I'd love to ride out and help with the mustering. I get so tired of just cooking all the time. Of course, I'll make sure the kitchen is covered. Betty and Joyce are planning to come, they can manage. Can I ride with you?"

"We can use all the help we can get. Appreciate your offer." He smiled again and touched the brim of his hat. "Come out later and show me which horse you like to ride."

She simpered.

Becca stared at her. Jealousy flared. She didn't want

Suzanne flirting with Josh. And she hated his flirting back.

No, he wasn't flirting, just being courteous. But it had the same effect. Suzanne looked like a cat with a canary.

"I thought you didn't like to mess with cattle," Becca said.

Suzanne turned her eyes toward her, a hint of anger showing briefly. "Why, Becca, this may be my last chance to help out on the ranch. I'll be leaving soon. It's really not my home any longer, so I don't feel I can exactly just drop in any time."

"You can. It is your home."

Suzanne ignored her and turned back to Josh, looping her arm in with his. "I never have worked in a muster before, but I can ride very well and am sure with a bit of instruction I can manage fine."

Slowly they walked out of the office.

Becca looked down. Bill Turner's letter was clenched in her fist. Slowly she relaxed her fingers and laid the letter on the hard surface of the desk. Smoothing the paper, she drew a deep breath. She refused to be jealous of her sister.

Reaching for the phone, Becca tried to ignore the incident just as Suzanne had ignored her for the past two days.

In seconds she had Bill Turner on the line.

Saturday morning dawned sunny and mild. After the late spring rains, the sunshine was a welcome change. Becca breakfasted standing by the counter, impatient to begin. She wanted everything to go well. Reviewing the plans, she saw no reason to doubt it'd be a smooth muster.

Suzanne joined her as she prepared to leave.

"I'll be out after I eat," she said. "Joyce will here any minute. She knows where everything is."

"We'll be leaving in a half hour. If you aren't there, we'll leave without you," Becca said, finishing the last of her tea.

"I'll be there."

The men were already at work when Becca reached the barn. Horses had been saddled, supplies laid in saddlebags. The activity was augmented when cowboys from neighboring ranches pulled into the yard. Unloading their own mounts, they called to each other, bragging on the work they could do in a day.

Becca loved the excitement, the camaraderie she experienced around neighbors she'd known her entire life.

Not surprising, Josh fit right in. He introduced himself to the new arrivals, told them who they'd be paired with, and outlined the plan for the next couple of days.

Becca mingled, thanking everyone for the help, catching up on news. She didn't speak directly to Josh, but she knew where he stood every minute. Twice she almost brushed against him.

Suzanne joined the group well before they were ready to ride. She greeted everyone in a friendly manner, but kept walking until she stood beside Josh.

Becca turned away. She didn't want to see Josh's expression as he talked with Suzanne. She needed to concentrate on the job at hand. Time enough later to worry about some attraction between her foreman and her sister— and the fact it bothered her.

"Ready to ride?" Josh came up to her.

"Yes. Let's do it."

He walked beside her as she went to her horse. Without a word, he lifted her into the saddle.

"I can manage," she snapped, immediately scanning the area to see if anyone had noticed. Only Suzanne's hostile gaze met her own.

"Never said you couldn't. See you back here before dark."

"Right. Who's going with me?"

It seemed a little odd to have to ask. She'd been in charge for so long. For once she liked not having to think, not worry about the logistics. Besides, she rationalized, it was good to see how Josh handled things. If she was serious about taking a few trips, she needed to know her ranch would be in good hands while she traveled.

"Head out, the ones assigned to you will follow. Trent and Mike from the Lazy M, the rest are from the other ranches."

"Okay. Take care."

He smiled that lazy smile that drove her crazy. His hand rested briefly on her thigh, heating her through the denim. "You take care yourself, Becca. Go get 'em."

She smiled and squeezed her legs around her horse. He started off. Josh wasn't one to mollycoddle her. She liked that. He knew she knew what she was doing and counted on her to pull her weight.

The warm glow in her heart lasted until she glanced back and saw Suzanne's horse right beside Josh's.

Of course Suzanne planned to ride with Josh.

Becca looked forward and kicked her horse. The sooner they got started, the sooner they'd be done.

By Tuesday afternoon, Becca was exhausted. She'd

worked long hours, rode until her bottom was numb, and kept a determinedly friendly attitude for everyone she came in contact with.

Except Josh and Suzanne. The two of them seemed inseparable. Suzanne was Josh's shadow.

Falling into bed each night, Becca took a long time falling asleep as she imagined her sister and her foreman together.

She relived Josh's kisses and wondered if he now kissed Suzanne. Wondered if he sweet-talked Suzanne in the dark of night.

But mostly she wondered at her own reaction. Confusion reigned. She didn't know what she wanted—a chance to travel, maybe to resume her college studies?

She'd soon have some money. Josh was capable of running the ranch in her absence. He'd more than proved that.

Yet was she tempted to stay—to spend time with a cowboy who wanted nothing long term. Was it because she reminded him of his past?

Long hours of contemplation in the dark of night didn't provide the answer, only left her short on sleep.

And so she was tired.

"Well, missy, looks like we both benefit from the deal."

Bill Turner joined her as she stood watching the last of the cattle being herded into the livestock truck. The hard work paid off. They finished loading the last steer late Tuesday afternoon.

Becca smiled at the older man.

"I'm glad you're happy. You are getting some good cattle."

"I know that. That foreman of yours drives a hard bargain. Don't know how much I'll make on the deal."

"No use talking poor mouth, Bill. The deal's set in concrete," Josh said, joining them. He nodded to the truck. "That's the last of them. You going to come out next fall and check out what we might be shipping then?"

"Sure am, if only to see if I can get a sweeter deal," Bill replied gruffly.

"You made out like a bandit and you know it," Josh said, settling his hat on his head.

He winked at Becca.

Becca smiled at the banter between them, her heart lifting at Josh's friendly gesture. For once Suzanne was not hanging around.

"Here you go, young lady." Bill reached into his pocket and pulled out a folded check.

Becca took it and looked at it, her eyes widening in shock. The amount shown was even more than she expected. And thousands more than she'd ever received from Sam Stuart.

Josh slapped Bill on the back. "Want to go into town for a celebratory drink or two?" he asked.

"Not today, young fellow. I've got some more business to attend to. Let me take a rain check." Bill looked over at Becca. "Take the young lady out, why don't you?"

"Tomorrow night I'm taking her to dinner. She's too tired today. But she can rest up this evening and even take a nap tomorrow if she wants," Josh said, watching Becca as he spoke.

Flushing slightly, she took a deep breath. "I'd love to go to dinner tomorrow, if invited, that is."

Her heart sped up. A date—was Josh asking her for a date?

"My dear Ms. Montgomery, it would be my pleasure to take you to dinner tomorrow night in celebration of a very successful spring cattle sale. Will you come?"

"Thank you kindly, sir. I accept. At what time should I be ready?"

He tipped his hat back and grinned at her formal response to his teasing. "I'd say about six. That will give us time to get there before we expire from hunger."

"Call me when you're in Cheyenne, son." Bill held out his hand.

Farewells said, Bill climbed into his car and drove away. Becca stood beside Josh, loath to leave. It was the first time in four days they were alone.

She looked at the check again. "I can't believe this. Josh, what would I have done without you? This is more money than—"

"If spending money's a problem for you, you could share a bit with your brother and sister," Suzanne said, walking up to Becca. She craned her neck to see the check, her own eyes widening.

"Good grief, who did you sleep with to get that amount?"

Becca flushed at her sister's crudely worded question. Slowly she folded the check and jammed it into her pocket.

"Bill offered a fair price for the beef," Josh said, frowning at Suzanne. "It was a clean business deal all the way around. You have no call to talk to Becca like that."

"It's the shock," Suzanne said, summoning up a smile. "And she knew I was teasing. We all know Becca doesn't have time to date. She's too caught up running her daddy's ranch. But with a check that size I'd think you could at least spring for some champagne to celebrate the sale."

"I could," Becca said.

The thought of sharing the champagne with the men who worked so hard brightened her spirits.

"We'll pick some up tomorrow when we're in town," Josh said.

"You're going to town tomorrow?" Suzanne asked sharply.

"I'm taking Becca out to dinner to celebrate."

"I want to come."

"No, this is for Becca," Josh said firmly.

Suzanne glared at her stepsister. "Sure, keep the boss happy, Josh. I'll see you later."

With a toss of her head, she stormed away.

"She could have come, too," Becca said slowly, unhappy with Suzanne's comment about keeping the boss happy. Was that the only reason Josh asked her out?

"No. This is for you. You deserve a night away from the ranch on your own."

"If this is some charity date because—"

"Blast it, you've got as bad a mouth as your sister!" Josh interrupted. He stepped forward, causing Becca to tilt her head back to maintain eye contact. "I want to take you out. Don't make such a production about it. You already said you'd come with me. End of discussion."

She wanted to explain, wanted to clear things up so he wasn't mad. But he turned and walked away, his back ramrod straight, his pace long and quick.

"Should I dress up?" she called, hoping she hadn't

angered him enough to change his mind.

Josh paused and looked over his shoulder. "We'll try that rib place in town. Jeans are fine."

So much for some elegant date, she thought, watching him as he entered the barn. She'd have loved candlelight and fine wine. Maybe a soft combo playing for dancing after dinner.

If they went to the barbecue rib place in town, they'd probably be home by eight o'clock.

Heading for the house, Becca's spirits bubbled.

Suzanne was right; she normally didn't date. Josh would be the first in years. And even if they did go in for ribs, she could still enjoy herself, forget about the ranch for a few hours, and devote herself to pure fun.

Having one of the county's most gorgeous cowboys as escort wouldn't hurt a bit, either!

Eight

The next morning Becca drove into town. She made the bank her first stop. She didn't want to delay depositing the large check. It was a relief to have a healthy bank balance.

Standing on the sidewalk, she debated her other errands. Giving in to impulse, she turned toward the heart of town. Sally Jean's was the main Western store in town. They had everything from boots to saddles, hoof picks to fancy Stetsons—and a complete line of Western wear.

"Hey, Becca, I haven't seen you in ages. What can I help you with?" Sally herself greeted Becca when she entered.

Weekday mornings were slow. Becca glanced around, relieved to find herself the only customer.

"Hi, Sally. I was in town and thought I'd drop by. Need a few things."

Becca felt the heat rise in her cheeks. She felt uncomfortable. She'd never bought clothes to impress a man before.

"Sure thing, just browse to your heart's content. Let me know if I can show you anything."

"Actually, I was sort of looking for a nice blouse. Something fancy, but not too fancy to wear with jeans."

"Mmm. hot date?" Sally asked with a teasing grin.

Becca's cheeks bloomed with color. Nodding, she tried desperately to pretend it was a common occurrence.

"I've got just the thing. Come on."

Sally led the way to the back of the store. Pushing hangers around the round rack, she found a lacy blouse. Pulling it off, she held it up for Becca. "Try this. It reminds me of old-fashioned girls."

Becca tried it on. It was lovely. Long sleeves with a trace of lace at the cuff. The high neck repeated the lace teaser, with a lace shield panel in the front providing the soft feminine look she wanted. Paired with her jeans, it looked beguiling. Slowly she smiled. It would do.

"Honey, you need new jeans. Those are faded," Sally said when Becca came out to show her the blouse. "And if you want to make a real impression on the man, let me give you a couple of hints."

By the time Becca returned to the Lazy M, her heart raced in anticipation. She had new clothes, makeup tips and newly pierced ears.

Leaning sideways, she glanced in the mirror again, smiling in delight at the gold earrings. She could scarcely wait until tonight.

A mistake. It had been a mistake inviting Becca to dinner, Josh thought as he watched her descend the steps that evening. She wore a pair of jeans that were so snug he wondered how she zipped them up. They molded her figure like a second skin, outlining the smooth curves of her hips, the seductive length of her legs.

The lacy white blouse looked as demure as a Victorian

lady's, but accented her femininity until he wanted to yank her into his arms and kiss her to make sure she was real. To feel the sweet softness of her body against his, feel the flames that raged when he touched her.

She'd piled her hair up on her head, tied in some sort of soft scrunch scarf, only a few tendrils drifted down to brush against her cheek. His fingers longed to push them behind her ears, skim that soft blushing skin. Her eyes sparkled, her lips tilted in a sensuous smile that had his own lips craving the taste of her again.

His glance was caught by the sparkle of gold in her ears. He hadn't known she wore earrings. It was the final sexy touch to an exquisite woman. Did she have a clue how much he wanted to snatch her up, carry her away to some dark, quiet place and make love to her until dawn?

He frowned.

He needed to remember his goal. Getting tangled up with some woman was not a step in his plan, no matter how enticing. The situation was too similar to the one he'd already been through. He'd learned his lesson from Tiffany. Unless the lady was willing to hand over a portion of her ranch, he wasn't interested. Tonight was to celebrate the sale, nothing more.

"Hello, Josh. You're right on time." Becca smiled warmly.

He cleared his throat, conscious of Suzanne coming out of the living room to stare at her stepsister.

"Good grief, Becca, pulling out all stops, aren't you?" she said scathingly.

"I think you look—"

His mind went blank. All he could think of was kissing

those rosy lips until the lipstick was gone and her color came from his mouth.

"Nice."

"Why, thank you, Josh. I'm glad you think so."

For a split second Becca was disappointed in the mild compliment. But a look at the raw hunger in his eyes made up for the innocuous word. She smiled again.

Suzanne ran her gaze over Becca. "Where are you going?"

"Robbie's Ribs," Josh answered easily, moving his gaze from Becca to look at Suzanne.

It was easier. He didn't feel the attraction to Suzanne as he did Becca.

"Mick Barnett is taking me out dancing. Stop by the O.K. Corral after you eat, why don't you?" she invited. "Join us."

"We might," Josh replied. He turned back to Becca. "All set?"

She nodded, holding her smile in place with real effort.

She didn't want to go to the O.K. Corral. She knew Suzanne would make a big production of having them sit together. Then she would flirt furiously with Josh, never forgetting to string Mick along at the same time.

Becca wanted Josh all to herself. Just for one evening. Was that too much to expect? Besides, she didn't want to go dancing. She hadn't been in six years. No, that wasn't right. She'd danced when the McFarlanes held that barn dance a few years back. But not with anyone important.

And Josh was important. Suddenly Becca held her breath.

She didn't want him to be. She wanted to cut loose from

the ranch, make her dreams come true and travel. Anything between them had to be temporary. She refused to tie herself down any more than she already was. She needed to be free, yearned to fulfill her dreams.

For the first time since her father died, she had a real chance. She wasn't going to jeopardize it.

"Hungry?" Josh asked as they walked out into the late afternoon sun.

The scent of hay and horses mingled with the fresh breeze blowing down from the mountain peaks. He opened the passenger door to his truck and waited while Becca climbed in.

"Yes. I ate a light lunch in anticipation of Robbie's Ribs. They're world famous, you know."

"I didn't. How did I miss that?" he asked, leaning casually against the open door.

She smiled. "Maybe Robbie's fame isn't quite as widespread as he says. How did you know about the place?"

"The men in the bunkhouse were unanimous in their recommendation."

"You told them you were taking me out?"

For a moment she didn't know whether to be annoyed or not. She'd never dated one of the ranch's employees.

"Sure, is it a secret?" He cut her a quick glance.

She sat up straighter. "No."

She wouldn't mind the whole town knowing Josh Randall asked her out. It was only dinner.

In moments he'd joined her in the truck and started for town.

"Tell me something about your dad," Josh said as he turned onto the highway.

"My father?" Becca was surprised. "What do you want to know?"

"Just tell me about him. What do you remember most?"

"He loved to laugh. And he loved the land. He never minded the freezing weather in winter or the heat in summer. He spent most of his life outdoors. He liked horses better than cattle, but felt there was more money in beef. Couldn't abide sheep, however, just like cattlemen of the Old West."

Josh nodded. "I've met a few like that even in these times. Has this ranch been in your family a long time?"

"My dad's uncle left it to him. He died in the war. My grandfather was a large animal vet. He didn't own a ranch, but worked on them his whole life. I think that's where Dad caught the bug."

"All your family gone now?" Josh asked gently.

"All gone. My mother died when I was a toddler. Gramma Mary took care of me until she died when I was in first grade. Then Dad hired a series of housekeepers to watch me. Until he met Eileen and married her."

"And did you like your stepmother?"

Becca shrugged.

"She's nice enough. She loved my dad. Didn't like the ranch, but put up with it to be with him. She made him happy and I'll always remember that."

"Not a bad comment on a person."

"What about you? What happened to your folks?"

She was greedy for information. She wanted to savor every morsel she learned. They had time to get to know one another, but would she have as much time as she wanted?

"My dad died when I was a baby. I don't remember a thing about him, except my mama loved him." He fell silent as the buildings on the edge of town came into view. "And that came from her. She never quite got over his death."

"And your mother?" she prodded.

"She died when I was in high school. Breast cancer. It was awful. She hated to leave me alone. She was the warmest, most loving woman I ever knew. Everyone loved being with her. I still miss her and it's been fifteen years."

"I don't think we ever get over missing loved ones. It just gets easier to go on alone as time moves along."

As she'd soon know. Suzanne planned to leave; Marc had already left. She'd better get used to it.

"In the final analysis, you can only count on yourself," Josh said.

She knew he was thinking about Tiffany selling the ranch after he'd worked so hard. Thinking how a betrayal like that would be hard to recover from.

"Sometimes you can count on your friends," she offered.

She hated the bitter tone in his voice. She wanted the evening to be lighthearted and fun. It didn't seem to be starting out too auspiciously.

"Where did you live after your mother died?" she asked.

"She'd been the housekeeper on a ranch in Colorado. When I started high school, the owner offered me part-time work. I continued living in our rooms until I graduated. Then went to work for him full-time for a couple of years. When itchy feet proved too much, I left."

She wanted to reach out and comfort a young boy whose last relative died leaving him alone at seventeen. She'd been twenty when her dad died. And she had her stepmother and brother and sister. Even if they didn't want the same things

133

now, when her father first died, they'd been there for her.

"Tell me every place you went, every exciting thing you've done. I'm going to travel one day. I'm going to leave Wyoming and see things!" she vowed.

"Like Key West."

"That'll probably be first. Or maybe New York City will be first. Or even San Francisco. There's so much I want to see, I don't know where to begin."

"You could travel all your life and not see everything."

"I know. But at least I'd see something besides the back end of a cow."

He laughed and reached over to take her hand in his. Threading his fingers through hers, he rested their linked hands against the side of the wheel. "Come with me to Cheyenne this weekend, Becca. We'll look at things besides cattle."

She held her breath, the thought of a weekend with Josh almost beyond imagining. They would eat at a fine restaurant. Maybe dress up and go to a nightclub and dance. Not like dancing at the O.K. Corral. They'd stay at a fancy hotel, have room service—

Slowly she shook her head. This time she thought before she spoke, but the answer remained the same. "I can't."

"A rain check?" he asked.

"I—maybe," she murmured, wondering why he'd asked her.

She wasn't the type to drive men wild, nor the type to go in for casual affairs. And despite her impetuous marriage suggestion a few days ago, she didn't want to be tied to a rancher. She needed to be free.

Two minutes later Josh turned into the parking lot

adjacent to Robbie's Ribs. The place was crowded for a Wednesday night. Still they found a table without any trouble. Becca knew quite a few of the patrons and waved or called a greeting as she followed the waitress to the empty table.

Conscious of their speculative glances, she met their gazes proudly. She knew people would be curious about her companion, but she didn't want to talk to anyone. She wanted the evening to be spent with Josh alone.

Becca determined to give Josh a date to remember. Once their order was placed, she told him stories about her childhood, funny ones, and ones where she'd learned something important, sharing with him episodes of her life that she rarely talked about.

He reciprocated and told her about working on the Colorado ranch, about competing in rodeos and about seeing the Pacific Ocean.

He chose his words carefully, intrigued by the shimmering light in her eyes when he spoke of a place she dreamed about. For a moment he considered going with her when she traveled.

Seeing the world from her eyes would bring it into a rosy focus he'd missed on his own.

But he'd knocked around enough. He wasn't getting any younger and he had his own dreams and goals to pursue. No matter how much he wanted to see the sparkle in Becca's eyes, he had to work for his ranch. It was too important to get sidetracked.

Becca took special care to keep barbecue sauce from splashing on her new clothes. The stretch jeans were comfortable, the blouse made her feel sexy and feminine. She cherished the memory of the look in Josh's eyes when he'd first seen her that evening. It warmed her like nothing else ever had.

For a moment she wished things were different. That she didn't want to leave. That he already had his ranch. Any interest between them would then be strictly personal, with no hidden agendas.

"Ready to go dancing?" he asked later as the waitress delivered the check.

Becca's happiness fled. Nervousness replaced the easy flow of conversation.

"I don't dance very well," she said slowly. "Suzanne's right. I don't date much and haven't had any practice over the last few years."

He shrugged, glancing at the bill. "We're not going to be in any contests. You can two-step, I'm sure. Everyone can two-step. We'll sit out the rest, if you like."

She rose when he did, reluctant to end the evening, but not looking forward to going to the O.K. Corral where Suzanne would be holding court.

Pretty, blond Suzanne, just the type Josh had married.

"I don't want to cramp your style. If you want to dance, you can," she said as they walked out to the truck.

"Meaning?"

"I'm sure you're used to dancing with lots of women."

He nodded. "After rodeo events there's always a few dances. The girls who like cowboys make themselves very available as partners."

"In more ways than one," she mumbled.

"Pardon?" Josh slowed down and looked at her. "Say again, Becca."

She shook her head. "It was nothing. I just meant you're probably a lot more experienced at this than I am."

"At dancing?"

His fingers caught her chin, turning her face up to his. The afternoon light had faded, twilight blanketed the sky. The light from passing cars illuminated them.

"Yes, at dancing. Among other things."

One side of his mouth curled up in a smile. "Such as?"

Her eyes locked with his, heat curled inside her. Her heart fluttered. His hand on her shoulder anchored her yet she wouldn't have moved an inch.

"You know perfectly well such as."

"Yeah, but I want to hear you say it."

He brushed his lips across hers, his eyes never closing, holding her gaze as he kissed her lightly again and again.

Straightening, he slipped his hand down to hers and linked their fingers again as he started walking to the truck.

"We'll dance with each other. We're out tonight to celebrate your sale. What's a celebration if we don't cut loose and have some fun?"

Resigned to going to the local nightspot, Becca nodded. It'd only be for a few hours. She could endure anything for a few hours.

The music from the country-western band at the O.K. Corral was blaring when they pulled into the parking lot. Loud, pumping, heart-rocking, it had Becca moving to the beat before she climbed out of the truck. Josh settled his hat, placing one hand at the small of her back and headed for the front door.

Inside, couples crowded the wooden dance floor, the tables surrounding the perimeter pushed around as groups congregated together. The music seemed even louder inside, but Becca didn't care. She'd be the perfect date and let him think she enjoyed this. Hr genuinely wanted her to have a good time.

The beat was insidious, suddenly she wanted to move her body in tempo, give up the cares of running a ranch for the evening and really enjoy herself.

"Let's go."

He took her hand and led her to the dance floor. In two seconds they were moving together, feet stomping, hips moving, smiles spreading. It was fun!

He could dance, she thought. His body moved on command, lithe, supple, and masculine. His eyes never left hers and the expression was pure male. He wanted her and he refused to hide the fact. His body hovered over hers, brushing against her, touching hers, tempting her until she wanted to throw herself in his arms and demand he never let her go.

The beat increased, the air grew hot and humid. Her blood raced through her body, heating her to a flash point. Yet Josh's gaze blazed even hotter. She couldn't look away, could only answer with her own hot look of desire, which she knew must be clearly visible.

Abruptly the song ended. Josh didn't move. He stood so close she felt almost captive. His breathing came hard, fast. His gaze hot, intense. She gulped for air, wishing they could sit down, go outside, do something to cool the heat.

The band segued into a slow, bluesy number. The light, already dim, faded even more.

Josh reached out to draw her slowly into his embrace, settling her body against him. She felt his hard planes, the strong muscles holding her, the heat from the recent exertion. His legs moved against hers as he rested his cheek on the top of her hair. The beat was so slow they could almost stand rock still and keep the tempo.

She'd never felt so gloriously alive.

She reached up to encircle his neck with her arms, her fingers toying with his hair. The hat was in her way, but she knew better than to expect a cowboy to take off his hat at a dance.

Smiling in complete contentment, she pressed closer in the intimacy of the dance.

"You look pretty tonight," he murmured in her ear. "Soft, feminine, almost virginal."

She stumbled, leaned heavily against him as her face flamed.

Josh pulled back and looked at her, realization dawning.

"Say one word, Randall, and you'll sing soprano," she warned at the light in his eyes.

"Honey, I think I'm charmed. In this day and age? You're what, twenty-six? Twenty-seven?"

"Twenty-six. I don't want to discuss it at all!"

He smiled and lowered his head until his forehead rested against hers, the brim of his hat resting on top of her head. Slowly he turned them around, his hands kneading her back.

"I knew you weren't the one-night-stand type. You're for love and marriage and babies, a white picket fence and family dog, the whole works."

"No, I'm for footloose and fancy free. Traveling wherever the whim takes me," she protested.

"Right," he said, as if he didn't believe a word she said.

When the music stopped, the band called a break. The

lights went back up and Becca stepped back. Blinking in the sudden brightness, she looked around for a table where they could sit and order some drinks. She was hot and it wasn't only because of dancing.

"Becca! Over here."

Turning at the familiar voice, Becca's heart dropped. Suzanne had saved places at the table crowded with her friends. There were two chairs free.

"Your call," Josh said, his hand on her shoulder.

She noticed he had touched her all night long. As if staking a claim. Or as if he couldn't bear to be separated from her. She liked it. She'd never had a date so attentive.

But that would change once they joined Suzanne.

"I guess we should sit with her, she saved the chairs and all."

"Your call," he repeated. But as she started to walk toward the table, he leaned over and kissed her mouth.

"Yeeeha!" a cowboy called, spying the kiss.

"Marking my territory," Josh said in a low voice.

They were introduced to the others at Suzanne's table, ordered drinks and began to join the casual conversation. Most of the men were younger than Becca. All of the women were. These were Suzanne's friends.

When the conversation veered away from the newcomers, Suzanne leaned over Josh, practically climbing into his lap.

"Aren't you two the cozy duo," she commented.

Her red blouse was undone enough that the dark lace of her black bra was visible when she leaned over, which she did with aplomb.

Becca wanted to button the blouse to the collar and

demand her younger sister get home. She glanced at Suzanne's glass and wondered what she was drinking. She wouldn't be twenty-one for another—

Her birthday was Saturday.

With stark realization, Becca knew she'd done nothing about the party she'd promised.

How could she have forgotten Suzanne's twenty-first birthday? It was a milestone, an event for celebration. Could she arrange a party on short notice? How could she have forgotten her sister's birthday?

"Something wrong?" Josh asked, tilting his chair back, as if putting some distance between himself and the two sisters.

"Suzanne, your birthday is Saturday—" Becca began.

"Is that supposed to be a news flash? I know that."

She frowned at Josh, scooted her chair closer.

"I wanted to give you a party," Becca said.

"I told you I don't want one. I've made other plans." Her gaze slid to Josh, back to her sister. "In fact I'll be gone all weekend."

Before Becca could question her sister further on her plans, the band came back. Warming up for a line dance, they had people jumping up from their chairs and lining up on the dance floor.

"Come on, Josh, dance this one with me," Suzanne demanded.

"You don't need a partner for a line dance," he drawled, looking over the groups forming.

"Come on, it'll be fun. You don't care, do you, Becca? I know you don't know the steps, but I'll bet my last dollar Josh does," Suzanne coaxed.

He smiled at her and nodded.

"Then you should go. I'll finish my drink. Go on, Josh," Becca said, wishing with all her heart he would refuse.

"You sure you don't mind?" he asked, settling his chair down on all four legs.

"Not at all," she lied, the stiff smile almost cracking her cheeks.

"Come on!"

Suzanne rose and grabbed his arm, clinging as he stood and they walked to the dance floor. In seconds the familiar beat broke out and the line began to move in unison. When everyone stomped their foot, the rafters shook. When each member of the line moved synchronously, it was like watching poetry in motion. Up and back, turn to the left, sway and shimmy, hips moving, boots stomping.

Enviously Becca watched Josh. His face was alight with happiness. He knew every step, never made a mistake. And Suzanne moved right with him. Sometimes beside him, sometimes in front of him, sometimes behind him. Her tall body mimicking his movements as if they'd trained for years. They made a wonderful couple, Becca couldn't help but think. Both tall, she so fair, he so dark.

It went on endlessly.

Becca wanted to leave. She debated getting up and walking out. But she had no way home. And she refused to make a scene. The minutes would pass. She'd be home soon enough.

And never go out with him again!

When the song ended, Suzanne threw herself against Josh, his arms coming up automatically to steady her. He bent his head to hear what she had to say. Becca gripped her glass, resisting the urge to throw it across the room at the couple. Deliberately she looked away but not before she saw Josh look over Suzanne's shoulder.

"Want another Coke, honey?" The waitress stopped by.

"Yes, please."

Holding the glass gave her something to do.

"They're playing another one for us, Becca." Josh appeared by her chair.

"I'm getting a refill," she said, her eyes on the dancers, not on the disturbing man standing so close.

His hand came under her arm, half lifting her from the chair. "Don't sulk. I only danced one dance with Suzanne."

Outraged, she glared at him. "I'm not sulking!"

He grinned. "Doing a good imitation. Come on, this one you can do."

Smoothly he eased them onto the floor, couples already flowing in time with the lively Texas Two-Step.

They closed the place down.

Josh danced with Becca every dance, even teaching her the basics for the complicated line dances. Laughing and teasing her, he made sure she knew she was his date for the evening. He refused to dance again with Suzanne or any of the other ladies at their table.

Nine

Becca was delightfully tired when he assisted her into the truck. With the hard work on the roundup and the long evening, she looked forward to bed. She'd had a wonderful time. She even forgot the dance between Josh and Suzanne. The rest of the evening he'd devoted himself to her. She smiled at the happy memory.

They didn't speak on the ride home. The moon rode high in the sky, illuminating the hills in a magical silvery wash. Josh tuned in the radio and they listened to the country music, interrupted occasionally by static. The mountains cut off direct line and few stations came in clear all the time.

"I had a lovely evening," Becca said as he pulled the truck in beside the back door and cut the engine.

When he turned off the headlights, the darkness was instant. No lights shone from the house. The men in the bunkhouse had gone to bed hours ago.

"I'm glad you did, Becca. I wanted you to."

Josh turned slightly on the seat, resting his arm on the back, letting his fingers brush against her neck.

"We'll have to have another celebration when we have the fall roundup, if we do as well," she said breathlessly.

Staring straight ahead, she was unsure of what to do. She

should turn and kiss him goodnight. She'd had a wonderful time and the perfect ending to their date would be another of his kisses.

But she wasn't ready to end the evening.

"We don't have to wait that long, do we?"

His voice came soft. His hand encircled the nape of her neck and exerted pressure, drawing her across the bench seat, drawing her toward him.

She looked at him, able to see his silhouette in the faint starlight.

"I guess not."

"Good."

He took off his hat and placed it on the dash as he lowered his head and covered her lips with his own. His hands reached around her rib cage, drawing her even closer as he settled her against his chest and kissed her deeply.

The sweep of headlights filled the truck and Becca pulled back, squinting to see who had turned in.

"Your sister's timing is lousy. You need to talk to her about that," Josh grumbled.

He put on his hat and opened his door. Walking around the truck, he opened Becca's door just as Suzanne and Mick pulled up.

"You only beat us home by a few minutes," Suzanne said gaily. "Are you coming in for a nightcap, Josh?"

He looked down at Becca. "Not tonight." At the door to the kitchen, he tilted her head up with a crooked finger. "I'll see you in the morning." A feathery touch on her lips and he turned back to his truck.

Suzanne waved Mick off and waited by Josh's truck. When he reached her, she spoke softly. Becca stayed by the door, straining to hear what they said, but she couldn't.

Irritated with herself for caring, annoyed at Suzanne for returning at the precise moment she had, and at Josh for not extending the evening, she yanked the door open and entered the dark kitchen.

Not bothering with lights, she went straight up to her room. By the time she reached the window, Josh's truck was moving toward the bunkhouse. At least they hadn't had a lengthy discussion, she thought as she prepared for bed.

Maybe she should talk with Suzanne. Maybe she should warn her sister that she might be giving the appearance of pursuing Josh the way she threw herself at him whenever he was around.

Slipping beneath the covers, Becca knew she'd never advise her. Suzanne had forgotten more about men at her young age than Becca ever learned.

But it had been her that Josh had taken out. Her he danced with through the evening. Except for that one dance. She closed her eyes, her smile dreamy as she remembered the slow dances. And his teaching her to line dance. And the two-step.

It was inevitable that there would be a sense of letdown the following morning. The roundup and sale left everyone tired. The initial elation with the high sales figures already faded. Becca wrote bonus checks for the cowboys, a larger one for Josh. She'd never have received the increase in income if he hadn't insisted on the competitive bid process.

As she fingered his check, she wondered how much closer this brought him to buying his own ranch. It seemed almost self-defeating for her to give him extra money. It'd only hasten his departure.

She was only guaranteed until the end of summer. Time would fly.

The sky was a brilliant blue, the sunshine so bright it blinded. Becca tugged the brim of her hat low over her eyes to shade them from the glare as she headed for the barn. The air moved softly against her cheeks, bringing the tang of pine and cottonwood. Late spring in Wyoming was beautiful. For a moment she stopped and looked around, taking a deep breath of the scented air.

The hills were covered in lush green grass. Prime grazing feed. The recent rains had washed the dust from the house, the barn, the bunkhouse. Everything looked pristine.

A certain peace settled in her heart. Her father loved the Lazy M. And she loved it with a fierce possessiveness that startled her.

She loved it, but was it enough for her? For a lifetime? There was so much more to see.

And for so long she'd railed against the enforced stay at the ranch, making sure everything ran smoothly. Making sure she could earn enough from the ranch to keep it going and provide for Marc and Suzanne. She feared growing content and never taking her chance to live life the way she wanted.

Slowly she resumed walking to the barn. The bonus checks were tucked in her shirt pocket, she wanted them distributed this morning. Tomorrow most of the men would head for town after chores. With their unexpected bonus checks, it'd be a better weekend all around.

Entering the quiet barn, Becca paused a moment, waiting for her eyes to adjust to the dimmer light.

"Hi, Becca. Do something for you?" Jason came out of the tack room, a tangle of reins in one hand.

"I'm looking for Josh."

He was the foreman, she wanted him to give the checks. "Is he around?"

"He and the rest of the men are out on the range. I know he sent Trent to check the fencing over near the river. Don't know where the others are."

"I'll find him," she said, heading for Stoney's stall.

Still a bit stiff from the long hours riding during the muster, Becca worked out the kinks as she saddled her horse. Once clear of the barn, she urged him into a fast gait. The wind in her face brought a smile. Fresh and clear, the air cleared her mind. She was eager to see Josh again.

Not knowing where Josh was working, Becca began to make a sweep through the sections, going clockwise. After about an hour, she saw Mike. Riding over, she asked if he knew where Josh was. He did. Soon she was headed farther west.

She saw him when she crested the hill. He knelt on the ground, working with something. His horse stood nearby, patiently cropping the grass. Slowing her horse to a walk, she felt flustered, suddenly shy. She'd wanted to see him, but the urgency came from within. He'd return to the ranch house by dinner. She could have given him the checks then.

She hadn't wanted to wait.

When he heard the horse, he looked up. Spotting Becca, he stood and watched her draw closer. His hat shaded his face, his expression hard to read.

"Something up?" he asked when she rode close enough to hear him.

"Not really. What are you doing?" She pulled up and remained on the horse, gazing down at him. Her heart fluttered looking at him. For a moment she wondered if he saw through to her soul. He certainly must suspect why she'd come. Color stole into her cheeks.

"I found this tangle of rusted wire. I was tying it together so I can take it back to the homestead. I don't want any steers getting cut with it."

A small circle of barbed wire lay at his feet.

She dismounted easily, dropping her reins to ground hitch the horse. Looking around, she frowned. "Where did it come from? The nearest fence is half a mile away."

"Who knows?" He shrugged. "Probably been here for years judging by all the rust. It could have dropped off the truck last time someone repaired this section."

"Mmm."

She kept her gaze on the twisted wire, wishing she was brave enough to sashay over to him and tell him how much she had enjoyed herself last night. She'd love to smile up into his face until he leaned over and kissed her again.

Heat washed through her at the brazen thought.

"Becca?"

"Yes?"

She dared a look. His eyes matched the sky, blue and clear and mesmerizing. Then her mind shut down.

"Are you checking up on me?"

He took a step closer, his eyes wary, probing.

"Of course not, why would I want to do that?"

"I don't know. But the expression on your face suggests something's not right."

She tried to school her features to hide the emotions churning up inside. Blinking, she looked away, began to turn back toward her horse.

"Hey, remember what I told you about poker?" he said, resting a hard hand on her shoulder.

"That I give myself away every time?"

"You just don't have the ability to hide much. I'm sure it'll come with practice."

"And do I need to hide things from you?" she asked.

His left hand came up to her shoulder; slowly he pulled her closer.

"I don't know, Becca. What would you want to hide from me?"

She hesitated. Trembling with reaction to his touch, her gaze dropped to his mouth as if she could will him to kiss her again.

She needed to guard her emotions, guard her heart and throw up some protective barrier between them. He said he wasn't for her.

But she yearned for his kiss more than protecting herself from possible rejection. It was just a kiss.

"Maybe I'd want to hide the fact that I find myself wanting to be with you more than anyone," she said softly.

"No." He leaned over her until she felt surrounded by him.

"No?"

"It's the novelty. That's all. Nothing more."

She smiled tentatively. "Are you trying to convince me or you?"

"Both of us, I think." His grip tightened. "I like being with you, too."

Too much, he thought as he drew her slight body up against his. His hands slid down her back and he hugged her tightly. For a long moment he held her while he scanned the empty hills. The others had assigned chores, there was no reason for anyone to come over the hills. But he wanted to make sure they were alone before giving in to the desire that raged within him.

When her hands crept up to his neck, he pulled back far enough to capture her lips with his. The fiery heat that surged through him when she opened her mouth to his took his breath. He wanted her with an intensity that shocked him. She was young, innocent and provocative, and he didn't care. He wanted her.

Her hat fell to the grass, his joined it in only a second. The feel of her fingers threaded through his hair fed the need to feel those fingers all over his body. Just as he wanted to trace his own over all of hers, to test the soft texture of her skin, taste the sweetness, feel the pulsing warmth that didn't come from the sun.

Josh felt one of her hands move from his hair to the side of his face, tracing the ridges and planes of his features. Slowly her fingers trailed over his jaw and down his neck. He turned them around, taking small steps that would not break contact of her body with his. But if they fell down on the grass, he didn't want her near the barbed wire. Turning and turning, mimicking the dancing they'd done last night, he moved them farther and farther from the wire, the horses, their hats. Only the summer grass would cushion them if his legs gave way.

Her hand reached the barrier of his shirt and her fingers fumbled and released the first button. Josh's temperature skyrocketed when her hand slipped beneath the cotton and brushed against his muscles.

Smiling against her mouth, he brought his own hand around to match her actions. Her skin felt like warm velvet. His fingers paused on the pulse point at the base of her throat, feeling the rapid beat. It wasn't enough. He broke their kiss to taste her there, to feel the pounding of her heart against his lips and tongue.

He caught the sensual moan as she tilted her head to give him access, her hand momentarily stayed against his chest.

"Josh," she whispered, dragging her mouth across his cheek in a damp kiss, licking his jaw, rasping her tongue against his smooth skin.

"Mmm?"

She tasted as sweet as honey. She was as hot as a two-dollar pistol and she drove him crazy. He didn't know if he were spinning out of control or headed on a collision course with destiny. Her scent engulfed him as fresh and sweet as a spring garden.

Being with her was enough to drive a saint to sin. To make a man forget his vows, his promises and his goals and crave her until he died.

No!

Josh pulled back. She drove him wild. He almost forgot everything in his desire for her.

He released her and stepped back.

"Josh?"

Becca stared at him, stunned at the emotions that roiled inside her. She'd been in heaven, she knew it. His kisses drove conscious thoughts from her mind.

He stepped back as if she'd stung him.

"Josh? What happened?"

"You're enough to drive a man crazy," he muttered, pushing his fingers through his hair. "You could make a saint lose control."

"Is that bad?" she asked, scared at the sudden change. What'd gone wrong?

He lowered his hands and he looked at her. "Yeah, that's bad."

"Why?"

She didn't understand. How could something so wonderful be bad?

He reached out a hand as if to touch her, but when he saw what he was doing, he snatched it back. He walked to their hats and picked his up, placing it firmly on his head.

"I don't understand, Josh. Did I do something wrong?"

She was so new at this she could have done a dozen things wrong. But if he'd tell her, she could learn. Next time she'd do it right.

"No." He reached down for the coiled barbed wire and picked it up. "What do you want, Becca? An apology?"

"No, an explanation."

She stomped over to her hat and snatched it up. Holding it in front of her like a shield, she looked at him.

Blast everything, he wore his poker face again.

"It should be evident," he said.

"Well I'm a little slow today, explain it carefully in words of one syllable so even I'll understand."

He took a deep breath. "Becca, you're a beautiful woman."

She swallowed and stared at him. No one had ever called her beautiful before.

Suzanne was beautiful. The most she ever got before was cute.

Josh thought she was beautiful.

"But you want things I don't want. And I need things you can't give me. I'm not getting tangled up again with a woman who owns a ranch and needs someone to run it for her. I want a place of my own."

She turned away. She didn't want to hear it. What did that have to do kisses?

"You don't need some transient cowboy messing up your life," Josh continued.

"No. I don't," she agreed.

"I'm sorry things got out of hand."

Thoughtfully she scanned the sky. She felt the sting of tears, but blinked them away resolutely. "It was as much my fault as yours," she said honestly.

"I'll keep out of your way."

She turned back at that. "No need. What do you want from me, Josh? Is Suzanne right, do you want part of my ranch? Shall I deed a portion over to you?"

He glared at her, opened his mouth to speak, then snapped it shut and spun around. His stride was so heavy, his footsteps shook the ground.

Panic touched Becca. She liked spending time with Josh. And she learned from him. She needed him for however long he stayed.

"Don't leave," she cried softly.

She wanted to say something else, to rail against a fate

that let her glimpse heaven, then snatched it away. But she didn't.

She wisely said nothing. Slamming her hat onto her head, she walked to her horse.

"Oh, I almost forgot."

Reaching into her pocket, she pulled out the folded checks and turned toward him, her head held high. "Bonus checks, I thought you ought to pass them out. You're the foreman."

He took the checks, making sure he didn't touch her. "I'll pass them out tonight."

"Whenever."

She mounted and kicked her horse. She wanted to put as much distance between them as she could. Feeling like a total idiot, she wanted to out ride her thoughts and salve her battered emotions. From the heights of elation to the depths of embarrassment all in five minutes. A world record, surely.

She'd never felt so drawn to anyone like she did Josh Randall. He appealed to her on more than a purely physical level. He listened to her and taught her things she hadn't learned being on her own.

She liked his slow drawl and his easy manner of dealing with the men. They respected him and it showed.

His attention last night had been thrilling. Dancing had been more fun than she'd expected, and she wondered afresh if they'd ever go again.

Not likely. She'd be a fool to set herself up for heartbreak. And she sure as shooting didn't understand the man. One moment he was hot for her, the next he put her aside.

Was he angling for some kind of ownership interest? She

didn't believe it. She couldn't, yet he hadn't denied her accusation.

As soon as she put away her horse, she headed for the office. Pulling out the pamphlets and brochures of the various locales she dreamed about, she sat at the desk and began to make serious plans. The money from the spring sale would stretch a long way—including a vacation.

"I'll do the dishes tonight," Becca volunteered as she sopped up the last of the gravy with a segment of her biscuit.

"If you like," Suzanne said, leaning back in her chair.

"Dinner was great."

"Thanks."

Becca finished her ice tea, watching her sister. Surely they had more conversation between them than the stilted words they'd exchanged during dinner.

Suzanne was still upset that she had no legal interest in the Lazy M and didn't care that she showed that displeasure to Becca every chance she got.

Wishing for a return to the way things had been, Becca rose and gathered the dishes. As she rinsed them off and stacked the dishwasher, she wondered why things couldn't have gone on like she planned. If Marc had returned to the ranch, she'd have made him a part owner. Suzanne might have elected to remain and Becca could have deeded her a portion, as well.

Or her sister might have married, as Josh said, and not needed anything from the Lazy M.

Josh. If Marc had returned as planned she'd never have hired Josh.

Placing the last glass on the top rack, she wondered if she would really want to have missed the opportunity to know Josh Randall, no matter how she felt now.

Not that she was clear in that area—she'd never been so confused.

As if thinking about him conjured him up, Josh appeared in the doorway.

Suzanne spotted him first. "Josh, come in. You're in time for coffee."

She smiled sweetly and rose as if she would throw her arms around him. Becca turned, surprised.

"Won't be staying long, Suzanne. Thanks, anyway. We've got a poker game starting soon." He glanced at Becca. "Got a minute?"

"I'd love to join in. Marc taught me to play poker, so better watch out, I'm pretty good," Suzanne said, flirting.

Josh smiled and nodded. "We'll be warned. Go on down to the bunkhouse and tell the men to deal you in. I'll be there in a minute. I need to talk to Becca."

"Don't be long or there might not be anything left to win."

Suzanne threw a triumphant glance at her sister and left

"What did you need to see me about?" Becca asked, reaching out to dry her hands.

She wished the sink was still full, to give her something to do beside look at the sexy cowboy dominating her kitchen. And her thoughts.

"This." He fished the check from his pocket and held it out.

She looked at it, back at him. "What about it?"

"That's what I wanted to know. Look at the amount."

"I know the amount. It's a percentage of the difference in the income from what I expected from the sale," she said calmly.

"It's too much."

He continued to hold out the check as if he expected her to take it.

"It's not. I wouldn't have made all that money if I'd just sold to Sam again. You earned that money. You've made other changes around here that I never thought of. You know so much more about ranching than I do. As long as you stay, I need to learn all I can."

"It's part of my job, Becca. I don't need bribes to stay and work."

"It isn't a bribe."

"Then what is it? You're not making sense. On the one hand you say you want me to stay, and yet checks like this give me almost enough to head out on my own."

"And that's so important, isn't it?" she asked. "To be out on your own. Be careful, Josh, it's not all it's cracked up to be."

"What do you mean?" He lowered his hand, the check still held by the edge.

"I'm all alone. Marc's not coming back. Suzanne will be leaving soon. I've got more land than I need, but nothing else. It's a bit lonely. So be careful what you wish for, you might get it. And it might not be exactly what you want."

"It's what I want, all right."

"Good, then take the check. I feel you've earned it. You're that much closer to getting your precious ranch."

She tilted her chin and clamped down on the urge to say more.

"And with the additional money from this sale, you have enough to travel."

"That's right," she said brightly.

He looked as if he wanted to say more. She didn't care.

"You better get back to your poker game." She wanted him to leave.

He hesitated a moment. "Want to come?"

"No. I've other things to do."

Like wish she could play poker with him. Like wish the kisses on the range that morning hadn't ended like they had. Like wish he wasn't gun-shy around women who owned ranches.

Like wish she knew her own mind.

Josh spun around and left. Becca remained leaning against the counter until she knew her legs would support her. Slowly she walked up to her room. She felt tired, drained. Maybe an early night was what she needed.

But she didn't fall asleep. She lay in bed as the sky grew darker and darker, her thoughts mixed up and confusing. Tossing, she gazed up at the blank ceiling.

Later she heard Suzanne's laugh, heard the low murmur of voices drifting in her window. She couldn't hear the words, but she recognized Josh. Her sister laughed again and said goodnight.

Still Becca couldn't sleep. Finally she gave up and went down to the office. Nothing like bookkeeping and record updating to bore a person out of her mind. It was very late when she finally grew sleepy enough to go to bed.

Friday morning, Becca drove into town to get a birthday present for Suzanne. Because it was her twenty-first, a special event, she hunted for the perfect gift. When she saw the golden locket with a small diamond at the center, she knew her sister would love it.

Returning home. Becca mounted her horse and rode out to check on the fencing on the southern perimeter. She needed to keep busy and didn't want to be around anyone. Restless energy plagued her. Counting the hours until the afternoon, she knew Josh planned to head for Cheyenne for the weekend. The weekend he'd asked her to share with him.

Was it too late to change her mind? Maybe a weekend away from the responsibilities of the ranch would be exactly what she needed.

And they could have fun, their date proved that. The tension of the last day could be worked through.

They were both unattached. She could show him she didn't expect anything more than a casual friendship. She wasn't looking for love or marriage from him. That scared him and she didn't blame him after his experience with Tiffany. But she wasn't his ex-wife. He needed to see beyond Tiffany and take her, Becca, for who she was.

After all she had her own dreams. She was going to leave Wyoming and see the world.

But first she needed to decide if she dare risk a weekend with a wild and sexy cowboy.

She rode farther and farther away from the house, wishing again she could out ride her thoughts.

Deliberately staying away as long as she could drag it out, it was late afternoon by the time Becca returned to the barn. She unsaddled her horse and brushed him down. Turning him loose in the corral, she headed for the house. A shower was in order. After dinner, she'd sit outside. The evenings were growing milder and she found twilight the most pleasant time of day to sit and think.

Becca towel-dried her hair and pulled on her new jeans. Smiling at the snug fit, she searched for a top that provided a different image than her normal one. She didn't want to wear her lacy top around the house, but something different than the regular cotton shirts was called for. Finding a pink blouse, she pulled it on, pleased with the color that it gave her cheeks.

"'Bye, Becca, see you Sunday night," Suzanne called from the bottom of the stairs.

"Suzanne?"

Becca hurried to the stairs, only to hear the kitchen door slam shut. Whirling, she ran to her window. Before she could utter a sound, she stopped dead.

Suzanne smiled up into Josh's face, handing him her suitcase. He tossed it into the back of his truck. Right beside a duffel bag. Holding the passenger side door for her, he laughed at something she said.

Becca couldn't move. Suzanne was going with Josh? For the weekend?

She stared as Josh rounded the front of the truck and climbed in. In seconds they were gone, only the faint echo of the engine hovered in the air. Soon it faded and only silence remained.

The pain that pierced Becca had nothing to do with physical injury. Her heart felt bruised.

Josh had taken Suzanne to Cheyenne for the weekend? The weekend he'd first asked her to share? She couldn't believe it. Slowly she turned and sank onto the edge of her bed. What happened?

She thought he liked her more than that. She thought he

wanted to spend time with her, but was afraid of drawing too close because of Tiffany.

Maybe she'd misread the signs. Maybe he was only out for a good time with whatever woman would give him one. Or maybe he'd only been paying attention to her in hopes of acquiring part of the Lazy M. Now he'd given up.

It was full dark by the time Becca roused herself. She went downstairs to fix herself something to eat, but ended up dumping most of the sandwich in the garbage. Her appetite fled.

She should have said yes when Josh asked. He'd mentioned it more than once. She could have said yes any one of those times. Why hadn't she? Even that afternoon she'd considered—

She was glad she hadn't found him, hadn't said anything. How embarrassing if she had said yes after he'd already invited Suzanne.

The weekend dragged endlessly. Becca found herself watching the driveway to spot Josh's truck as soon as they returned, though she didn't know how she would face them—

Suzanne with her triumphant air of success and Josh with a pleased look on his face for a fabulous weekend. She really couldn't bear it. Partly because she wanted Josh for herself, partly because she had deliberately refused to take a chance for some fun and regretted it deeply.

Even her beloved pamphlets and guidebooks failed to hold her interest.

"You're a fool and a coward," she muttered as she tried to immerse herself in ranch work. Most of the men had taken the weekend off, either lazing around the ranch or visiting in town. They'd earned it after last week's muster.

But Becca refused to relax for a moment. Even working, her mind continued to imagine Suzanne and Josh together. She couldn't take the chance of what would happen if she sat down for a few moments.

Late Sunday night they returned. Becca heard the truck. She lay in bed, feeling numb. They didn't take long to say goodnight, she thought as Suzanne entered the kitchen a couple of minutes later. Humming to herself, she hurried up the stairs and into her room.

Becca pulled the covers over her head and tried to drive out the thoughts that wouldn't turn loose.

Ten

Becca braced herself the next morning when she heard Suzanne stirring. She prepared her breakfast as quietly as possible in order not to disturb her. She wasn't ready to hear about her sister's glorious weekend.

Suzanne drifted in, wearing a shockingly revealing gown and robe set. Becca stared.

"Nice, isn't it?" Suzanne purred. "A birthday present, of course. Don't you love it?"

She danced across the kitchen floor, twirling around so the diaphanous material floated about her. "Thank you for the locket. I found it on my pillow when I got in last night."

"Don't you think that's a bit revealing for wearing around here?" Becca asked, thinking instead of a locket she should have bought Suzanne some flannel pajamas. "Some of the men could wander in."

A touch of envy shot through her. She'd never owned anything as feminine and sexy as that negligee.

"Unlikely at this hour," Suzanne said, her eyes bright. "And even if anyone did come in, he probably wouldn't see anything he hasn't already seen."

Becca's face flamed. Was her sister suggesting—

"I have work to do." She slammed her cup down on the

counter and started for the door.

"Well of course you do, Becca, dear. That's all you have, isn't it? Your work." Suzanne's tone sounded sweet, but Becca knew the intent was anything but.

She turned and faced her. "I'm sorry your mother didn't want to hold on to any part of the ranch, Suzanne. I paid good money to buy her portion. She should have told you and Marc years ago. Don't take your anger out on me!"

Suzanne's eyes glittered, and she held on to her temper with obvious effort. "I have nothing to be angry about, Becca. After all I just spent a glorious weekend in Cheyenne. I'm glad I don't have a ranch hanging around my neck like an albatross. If a man asks me to go away for the weekend, I'm free to do just that. To enjoy myself and not make a martyr of myself for some dumb land!"

Becca felt as if she'd been slapped. Swallowing hard, she didn't know what to say. She stared at the girl who had shared her home for years, the younger girl who had been the sister Becca always wanted.

She saw only a selfish woman with a spiteful smile and hateful eyes.

Without a word, Becca turned and headed for the barn. She stumbled once and realized her eyes were full of tears. Brushing them impatiently away, she stopped. She couldn't run into any of the men with tears spilling down her cheeks. And she couldn't go back to the house and face Suzanne.

She was right. Becca felt a bit like a martyr, trying to hold on to a ranch that no one but she had an interest in.

She'd wanted to go away for the weekend, but fear had made her refuse.

Now she was upset and unhappy and didn't know where

to turn. What she really wanted was for Josh to come out to her. Gather her up in his arms and tell her the weekend had meant nothing, that he didn't care for Suzanne any more than he cared for her.

She almost smiled. That was not what she wanted to hear. She wanted him to tell her how much he loved her.

Shock held her immobile.

Love?

When did that happen?

Since when did she want love from her summer cowboy?

Forever, whispered her mind.

Since she'd first met him.

Since the first kiss.

Since the night they'd gone dancing.

Stifling a moan, she realized she'd fallen in love with him despite his warnings, despite his own caution, despite her own uncertainties as to the reasons for his attention.

That's why it hurt so badly when he'd taken Suzanne over the weekend. That's why she hadn't wanted him to stop kissing her in the field the other day. That's why their date last week had been so special.

She loved him.

Rubbing the ache in her chest, she spun around and headed for her truck. She couldn't face anyone right now. She needed some time to think this through.

She couldn't love a man who didn't love her back, could she?

Unrequited love was not uncommon. It was painful and hopeless, but not uncommon.

And wasn't it her luck to fall for a man who had made it

clear from the very first that he had no interest in a woman who owned a ranch. Everything else being equal, she couldn't change that fact.

Driving aimlessly, Becca found a turnout overlooking the Wind River and pulled the truck to the edge. The water spilled and splashed around the rocks as it rushed downstream. Except for the occasional car that passed on the highway, Becca was totally alone. The wind swept across the rocky crag, blowing through the truck windows.

She had trouble believing her own emotions. She didn't want to fall for some cowboy. She wanted adventure, excitement, to see new places.

Yet she'd fallen in love with a man who knew ranching and wanted to build his own.

How could she face him, knowing how she felt? Was she strong enough to hide it?

He'd said she gave everything away in her eyes. But not this. Time for a crash course in poker faces. She refused to reveal her feelings to anyone, not Josh, not Suzanne, no one.

Maybe it was merely infatuation. Maybe because he was the first man to attract her on a physical level she imagined more than there really was.

Maybe she needed something else to put this all in proper perspective.

She'd been talking about traveling all her life. Time to do something about it. As soon as she returned to the ranch, she'd make reservations. Nothing held her to the ranch. She had enough money to afford a trip. And she'd take it. Counting the months, she figured she could be gone three months until September.

Josh could handle things while she was gone. He'd

proven he knew more about ranching than she did. The men had no problem working for him.

How could she have so foolishly fallen for him despite his warnings?

It was mid-afternoon by the time Becca felt sufficiently under control to risk facing Josh. When she pulled up behind the house, he came from the barn.

"Where have you been?" he growled when she stepped out of the truck.

Becca bit back a quick none-of-your-business retort and shrugged. If she didn't meet his eyes, he couldn't guess. This much she'd decided when she sat by the river. "I had errands to run. What's up?"

She looked over toward the barn.

"I wanted to talk to you. Suzanne said you left early this morning."

She nodded.

"One of your mares is in season. You want to have her covered by Rampage?"

She almost looked at him then. It was hard to avoid. Especially when she longed to trace her gaze over his face, his broad shoulders, his arrogant cowboy walk.

"If I pay a stud fee," she said stiffly.

"Five hundred dollars."

"That's chicken feed, not a stud fee."

His gaze caught hers and he stared down at her as if analyzing something. "That's the fee."

"I'll take it. Thanks."

She knew what he was doing but wasn't going to stand around arguing about it. She'd be an idiot to refuse the offer of a fine stallion like Rampage. She turned away. She needed to get away. The urge to throw herself into his arms and kiss him gained strength as he stood so close beside her.

"Where are you going?" he asked.

"Inside, I've reservations to make."

"Becca?"

She glanced over her shoulder, looked to the left of him.

"I'm taking your advice, Josh and getting in some travel time while you're here."

She continued into the house.

When she reached the office, Suzanne sat perched on the edge of the desk, talking excitedly into the phone. She saw Becca and paused. "Becca just came in. I'll tell her," she said.

Holding the receiver away a few inches, she stood. "It's Marc. He's invited me to join him in California. I'm leaving."

"Good. I hope you both enjoy the state."

Suzanne held out the receiver. "Marc wants to talk to you," she said.

Becca hesitated, took a deep breath and took the phone. "Hello, Marc."

"Look, Becca, I've talked to Mom and gotten the full story from her. I...she said how much you've done for us when you didn't need to. I don't think I handled this situation so good. But I was afraid to come home and see you face-to-face. I thought once I was there, you'd find a way to keep me there and I really don't want to be a rancher."

"I'm sorry you didn't feel you could say something before," she said slowly.

"Yeah, I am, too. I, uh, Becca, you've always been great, just like Suzanne." He hesitated a long moment. "I guess what I'm trying to say is, I do think of you as my sister and

I...I love you."

She blinked her eyes and nodded. For a moment she couldn't speak around the lump in her throat. "Thanks, Marc, I love you, too."

"Come see us in California some time."

"Maybe I'll stop by and visit one day," Becca said.

She said goodbye and gently hung up.

"I'm leaving tomorrow," Suzanne said defiantly.

Becca nodded, saddened at the way things had turned out.

But that was life and she had exciting plans of her own. Maybe in the long run, this would prove to be a blessing.

"That's fine with me. I'll be leaving myself in a couple of days. I won't have to worry about you staying here alone."

"Where are you going?"

Suddenly Suzanne's expression changed. Suspicion replaced triumph.

"New York to start. Then Key West. Beyond that I'm not sure yet."

Suzanne looked at Becca as if she'd never seen her before.

"I want to go with you."

"No," Becca said firmly. "I'm going to do what I want for a change. Josh was right. Your mother took advantage of me. She should have been the one to take care of you and Marc during the last six years, not me. I'm too young to be stuck for the rest of my life on a ranch. I did it for our family. Only it got me nothing. You're leaving. Marc didn't even return to pack up his things. I'm tired of it."

Suzanne's eyes widened. "Becca, you've always loved the ranch."

"You don't know a thing about me, Suzanne," she said. "What I've always wanted to do is travel. I wanted to attend college in the worst way. I want to do a lot more with my life than herd cattle all day long. But you never knew that. You never even tried to find out."

"Maybe she didn't have a chance. Maybe you came across so strong and independent, she thought you liked ranching," Josh said from the office doorway.

"Figures you'd defend her," Becca muttered, crossing the room to stand by the window.

Suzanne didn't own a ranch. She was tall and blond and loved fun—much more Josh's type than a petite woman with a yen to travel.

"What do you mean by that crack?"

Josh came up right behind her.

She turned and almost bumped into him. Stepping back, she felt the edge of the sill press against her back. "Just I'm glad there is a bit of loyalty there. Maybe you aren't all cold and hard and uncaring."

"I'm not cold or hard. And I don't know about loyalty but I do know about being rational. Which you are not acting right now," Josh said.

Suzanne pushed Josh aside. "I want to go on the trip, Becca. You're using the money you made from the sale. I helped. Didn't I, Josh? I rode out every day. I coordinated the kitchen help. I deserve some of that money. I want to go with you."

"Well, I don't want you with me. Or anyone else for that matter. I want to be on my own for the first time in my life," Becca said calmly. She met Suzanne's gaze without flinching. "I'm not taking anyone with me."

"But I—"

"Leave it, Suzanne. Becca deserves some time to herself. And it's something she's waited for a long time," Josh said, his eyes never leaving Becca's face. "You've got your own life to live. Go to California and see if you like it there. If not, I'm sure you can always come back here."

Becca's gaze was truly caught. She felt herself sliding into oblivion in the depth of his dark blue eyes. She wanted to reach out and touch him, have him hold her, give her some of his strength. But she knew better.

Suzanne forgotten, Becca rallied her defenses to deal with Josh. Her sister could wait, this couldn't.

"Did you need to see me for something besides the mare?" Becca asked.

"I want to talk to your sister, Suzanne. Could I do so in private?" Josh asked. "Maybe you should get started on your packing if you're leaving tomorrow."

Once they were alone, he stepped closer, crowding Becca against the windowsill.

"There's something different about you today, Becca," he said.

Her eyes on his throat, she wondered if she could dash to the side and escape.

"I'm the same I've always been."

Except for falling in love. Was it so obvious?

"Then why are you as skittish as a newborn colt? Look at me."

She looked up, studying the firm lips drawn in a tight line, scanning the hollows of his cheeks. His finger tipped up her chin and her eyes met his.

"There's nothing different about me," she repeated.

"Maybe you're just seeing things that aren't there. Maybe a fun-filled weekend was more than you can handle."

His eyes narrowed. "Meaning?"

She knocked his hand away. "Meaning whatever it is you want it to mean."

"Do you wish you'd come with me?"

He began to smile.

"And cramp your style? Heaven forbid. I'm sure Suzanne proved to be much more entertaining than I could have been."

"Suzanne didn't spend the weekend with me. Did you think she had?" he said quietly, his eyes searching hers.

"You left together and returned together. You wanted someone to spend the weekend with. What do you think I thought?"

For a moment hope glimmered.

"I wanted to spend the weekend with you. Not Suzanne. I gave her a ride into Cheyenne, picked her up when I left. We spent about five hours together in the truck. That's all."

The relief that flooded through her almost buckled her knees. They hadn't spent the weekend together, not like she imagined.

"She's pretty," Becca said inanely.

"She's also young, and sowing wild oats. Let her go to California. She'll probably end up having a wonderful time."

"I'm not stopping her."

"No, you're ready to leave yourself, aren't you?"

"Yes. If you stay and run the place, I can take a trip."

"No problem. How long will you be gone?"

"Three months. Maybe longer. I don't know just yet."

"Three months!" He looked thunderstruck.

"Maybe longer. I'll have to see how I like it."

"Maybe you'll like it so much you won't want to return to the ranch."

He was right. As long as she felt like she did, she wanted to stay away from him. The ache in her heart grew with each passing moment.

She wanted him to love her, put her ahead of ranching and trust her love for him.

He never would. He'd been too burned by Tiffany.

"If I decide to sell, you can have first right to buy."

He frowned at her words. "What if I leave now?" he asked.

"Then I'd miss my trip."

Already the ache was growing. She didn't want to think. She didn't want to feel.

If she didn't take the chance to leave now, she might never have another. She'd been yearning to travel. Josh gave her the opportunity.

He stepped back, turned and walked toward the door.

"Take your trip, Becca. You've earned it. I'll take care of your ranch for you."

Alone, she stared at the empty doorway. He said nothing about her staying.

Slowly she walked to the desk and pulled the phone close. In moments she had a travel agent on the line.

She was leaving. He couldn't believe it. Yet he should have expected something like this.

She'd been talking about taking a trip since he'd first met her. And she deserved it. After raising her stepbrother and stepsister, she deserved some time on her own, doing what she dreamed of doing. Marc and Suzanne were ready to go out on their own. That freed Becca. Time for her to follow her dreams.

He was pursuing his dream. How could he begrudge Becca her own? He should take some satisfaction in knowing it was because of him she was able to afford to go. Able to leave her ranch in his capable hands and know it'd be in good shape when she returned.

He had some other ideas for improving things, but until he owned his own place, he wouldn't put them into effect.

Idly he wondered what Becca would say if he offered to buy into her ranch. Maybe if he waited long enough, he could buy it all. She wouldn't be back.

He lifted his hat and ran his fingers through his hair, gazing over the range. It was a nice spread. How could she bear to leave it?

He knew the lure of the city, of exotic places and different people. Tiffany had quickly succumbed when she'd left the ranch. She'd gone to work in New York and the last he had heard she loved it.

He didn't want Becca to be the same, but she was.

If the timing had been different, if he'd met Becca after he had his own place, things might be different. Once he owned his own place, if he wanted to take a trip, he'd save until he could afford one.

But he didn't own a place yet. And he'd spent too many years pursuing that goal to give up now. To give it up for a woman who wanted something else.

He'd let her go and hope to goodness she didn't meet anyone else before she decided whether to come home.

Maybe in a few years—

Who was he kidding? He didn't have a few years. As pretty as Becca was, he'd be lucky if the first man who saw her didn't snatch her up.

And if the man lived in New York or Key West, he'd have a lot more going for him than some itinerant cowboy seeking his own dream.

Eleven

Suzanne left the next morning. Becca insisted on driving her into town to catch the bus that would take her to Denver where she'd catch a flight to the west coast. Neither woman said much on the ride in. Becca regretted the loss of the easy conversations they had enjoyed in the past. She missed the hero worship she'd received when Suzanne had first come to the ranch and met her big sister.

Time changed everything.

The bus sat waiting when they pulled in. Suzanne bought her ticket, checked her luggage and started for the door. She glanced at Becca, then turned and threw her arms around her.

"Thanks for everything, Becca. I hope you find what you want. Come visit us. We'll show you the best California has to offer."

Becca hugged her tightly, then stepped back, her eyes bright with unshed tears.

"I hope you love it there, Suzanne. You're going to knock the guys right off their feet."

"If they don't think I'm some sort of hick. But I can learn fast. Bye."

She stepped on the bus. In a second she was back, an odd expression on her face.

"Becca, about last weekend. I let you think I went away with Josh, but he only gave me a ride. I met up with Marilee Chapman and we went shopping and eating and to the show. It was my birthday treat to myself. I spent the weekend with her. I overheard Josh invite you and when you refused I thought it a way to get back at you because of the ranch and the money and all." She took a breath. "I think he likes you. He certainly treats me like a kid."

"I thought you told me to watch out for him," Becca said, touched her sister wanted to clear things up before she left.

Suzanne hugged her quickly. "I did, but it was spite talking. He never tried to talk you into anything, did he?"

"No."

He never denied interest in the ranch, either.

"I've gotta go, Becca. I probably won't write much, but watch your email for any I send. And I'll text you or call from time to time. I'll let you know how cool LA is."

"Have fun. Enjoy every moment. I hope you find what you want. Bye, Suzanne."

Becca waved until the bus pulled away and was lost from view. She missed Suzanne already. For the last decade she'd lived with her sister, except for the few months she'd been away at college. Now Suzanne was gone, probably for good.

"But I'm leaving, too," she said as she walked back to the truck. "And on the first of many, many trips."

Somehow the excitement wasn't as strong as she'd anticipated.

Josh was waiting for her when she returned. He opened

the truck door for her.

"Suzanne get off all right?" he asked.

Becca nodded and slid from behind the wheel.

"When do you leave?"

"Friday morning, same bus," she said. "It'll take me to Denver and I'll get my flight from there in the afternoon."

He slammed the door so hard the truck rocked. She swung around and stared at him. "Something wrong?" she asked.

"No. But if you're leaving in a couple of days, we have a lot of work to do. You better show me the computer program you use, how you track everything. Give me signing authority and give me an idea of what you want me to do while you're gone."

"Then let's get started." She led the way to the office.

The next three days passed swiftly. Josh and Becca spent most of the time together. He wasn't familiar with her computer program for ranch records, but learned quickly.

He discussed long-range plans and short-term projects. They discussed the men who worked on the ranch and their compensation. Josh had new and innovative ideas regarding cattle feed and marketing.

He explained some different concepts of breeding and Becca agreed to let him try a few select heifers in an aggressive program.

Becca cherished every moment spent with Josh, storing up as many memories as she could to take with her. She lay awake long into the night remembering every word Josh said during the day. Remembering the way she caught him looking at her when she hadn't expected it. Remembering the way his hair grew long against his collar, and the way he ran his fingers through it when he became frustrated.

And she remembered the touches. Innocent, innocuous. He'd hand her a paper and brush against her fingers. He'd lean over the desk and skim her shoulder. When the breeze blew her hair, he'd tuck it behind her ear, lingering a second longer than necessary.

She'd gone to the bunkhouse to play poker one night. Keeping her face averted from him, not because of the game but because of the secret in her heart, she was annoyed that he still won.

Maybe she'd practice on her trip and when she returned home they could have a rematch before he left in September.

If she came back.

Tomorrow was Friday. Becca packed the last of her clothes in the single suitcase she planned to take. One of her fantasies was to buy a new wardrobe. She didn't want to be labeled "western rancher" by everyone who saw her.

She'd buy sophisticated dresses in New York and skimpy beach wear in Key West. But she'd take a couple of pairs of jeans for the days she wanted to be herself.

"Becca?" It was Josh calling from the kitchen.

She went to the top of the stairs. "I'm upstairs packing." In a moment he appeared at the bottom of the steps.

"Trent said you asked him to drive you into town tomorrow. I'm taking you," he said.

"You don't have to do that. Trent won't mind."

Her heart began pounding. It was one thing to slip out early in the morning without having to see Josh, something else entirely to have him be the one to see her off.

"I want to."

She stared down at him afraid the loneliness she dreaded showed in her face. She'd miss him so much! He'd become so important to her in such a short time.

But it was better this way. Being around him was a kind of torture she didn't enjoy. She'd miss him while she traveled, but at least there'd be no danger she'd give herself away.

He'd never said anything. Just kissed her like there was no tomorrow. But never said he cared for her.

She'd have all the new sights and experiences to take her mind off the cowboy who had stolen her heart and didn't even know it.

Josh climbed the stairs until he stood beside her. Without a word, he cupped her cheeks and tilted her head back. He kissed her gently.

Clutching his wrists, she opened her mouth and let him deepen the kiss. Tears gathered behind her lids. She loved him and he hadn't a clue. He wouldn't appreciate finding out, either.

She very much doubted she'd ever feel any differently. Unless she grew to love him even more.

He pulled back and she ducked her head, hiding the tears.

"Becca?"

"I'll be ready around seven. We can leave then," she said, staring at his boots.

He didn't move for a long time. Then said, "Seven it is. Goodnight."

He descended the stairs and left the house.

Becca dressed casually in a short navy skirt with a loose yellow top. She wore flat shoes and they felt odd after years in boots. She rarely dressed like this and for a moment was pleased Josh would see her in something other than jeans.

She opened her door and stopped. Josh leaned against the opposite wall.

"Came for your bag," he said, pushing away and heading straight into her room.

"I could have managed, but thanks." She gave her room a last sweep. She wouldn't be back for months. It seemed odd, knowing that.

She turned and started down the stairs. She'd wanted this for years. Why wasn't she happier?

The drive was as silent as her last drive with Suzanne. There were a dozen things she wanted to say but none were important.

The important thing, that she loved him, she couldn't say.

The bus waited. She swallowed when she saw it. Life's big adventure beckoned and she wished Josh would kiss her again. Tell her he cared for her. Ask her to stay.

"Got everything?" he asked instead.

"Yes. I'll call and let you know where I'm staying. If anything comes up, feel free to contact me. You have my cell number."

"I think I can manage, Becca. You have yourself a good time."

He handed the suitcase to the bus driver and placed his hand on the small of her back, steering her toward the open door.

"I'll take care of your ranch, honey. You take care of yourself."

"I will."

She couldn't look at him. Her heart felt as if it were breaking.

When he pulled her into his arms she clung tightly, not wanting to say goodbye.

I love you.

"Don't go falling for any other man in New York or Key West. You're a Wyoming girl. You come back home," he whispered in her ear.

She nodded. If he only knew there was no chance of her falling for anyone else. Ever.

"'Bye, Josh, thanks for the ride."

"Becca." He kissed her hard and stepped back, his blue eyes dark and stormy as he watched her board the bus. He followed her progress as she walked to a seat and sat beside the window. She smiled and waved, hoping the tint of the window kept the tears from showing.

"Goodbye my love," she said softly.

Twelve

Becca paced nervously in the small reception room. Trent would be here soon. She glanced at her watch. She'd called him almost an hour ago. Where was he?

She took a deep breath, gazing out the open window. She was surprised at how good it felt to be back in Wyoming.

She'd loved New York. The first week, that was. Well, maybe love was too strong. She'd been intrigued, fascinated, impressed.

Then the crowds got to her, making her feel closed in, insignificant. The glass and concrete of the city canyons didn't offer the freedom of the Wyoming ranges. The air was hot, humid and smelled of gasoline and humanity—not of dry grass, cottonwoods and the scent of cattle.

She'd spent a week in the nation's capital and visited museums and monuments and Arlington.

Key West had been all she expected. Peaceful, beautiful. And the ocean had been as warm as a bath. Salty, but clear and heavenly to swim in, unlike the cold tributaries of the Wind River.

She'd enjoyed herself there the most.

As much as she had enjoyed any time over the last five weeks.

She smiled at the receptionist again and leaned against the window frame. The older woman probably wondered why she couldn't sit still. But she was too excited. And a bit fearful. She contemplated the risk. While the outcome was uncertain, it was a risk she felt justified in taking. Though she was gambling a lot on one word.

The familiar ranch pickup truck pulled up in front of the attorney's office.

"My ride's here. Bye."

Becca grabbed her suitcases and headed for the door. Trent met her on the sidewalk and tossed her bags into the back.

"No one's expecting you, Becca. Your call sure surprised me," he said as he held the door to the passenger side open for her.

"You didn't tell anyone else that I called, did you?"

You didn't tell Josh, did you? She was counting on the element of surprise when he saw her to tell her what she needed to know.

"No, ma'am, didn't tell no one. Just hopped into the truck and drove in. What happened to your trip? We thought you would be gone a lot longer than this."

"I got homesick," she said briefly.

She touched her purse with the precious papers inside. Truer words had never been spoken. She'd ached to return home. Nothing had been as she had once thought it'd be. She'd missed everything.

Everyone.

Someone.

"Well, you won't find a prettier place on earth than the Wind River area," Trent said with authority.

185

She wasn't going to argue, but it wasn't the ranch or the area. Wherever Josh Randall hung his hat would be the prettiest place on earth for her.

The last five weeks had proved that beyond a doubt.

Traveling hadn't proved her love for Josh to be infatuation. It'd endured, grown, until she hadn't enjoyed a single moment away from him.

The longed-for travel had seemed flat. The sites she'd visited had been interesting, but without someone special to share her excitement, they hadn't seemed important.

But the nightly conversations with Josh had grown in importance. She called the first night to check in and let him know she got to New York safely. Then he'd said to call back in case he had any questions about the ranch. So she'd called most nights.

If she missed their normal time for the call, he'd call her.

And the ranch wasn't the only topic of conversation. They'd always start that way, but then she shared her experiences. Then he'd talk about any parallels in his life.

And before she knew it, they'd discussed their like of mystery books, comedy movies, Thanksgiving dinner and their mutual dislike of working in the rain. About updates from Suzanne and Marc, and how Rampage and Bonnie and the other horses were doing.

She watched as the familiar landscape raced by. Trent drove like all cowboys—fast, as if the bumps and potholes in the road were something to be got over as quick as possible. Bouncing and shimmying, the truck sped along.

Taking a deep breath, she wished the butterflies doing the cancan in her stomach would cease. She forced herself to concentrate on studying the hills, estimating how much grazing remained for the year. She was up to speed on the harvest plans for hay. The tentative plans for the fall muster.

"Heard anything from Suzanne?" Trent asked, ignoring the rough ride.

"She sent a few emails. She likes California. She's getting a tan at the beach."

Becca smiled as she remembered the late-night calls with Josh when she'd told him about Suzanne's emails. California wasn't quite what she expected, but she'd found a job as a receptionist and they went to the beach every weekend.

The calls had been a lifeline to Wyoming. She hated to hang up when the time came each night.

He seemed to enjoy talking to her. Even said once that he missed her, then turned it off as a joke. But he'd repeated his admonition that she not fall for any slick city dudes. The husky tone to his voice gave her hope.

And that one word.

She hoped she wasn't making too much of the word, but it seemed important to her. The most important thing in her life right now.

She was counting on that.

Actually she was counting on a lot of things. Maybe she had it all wrong. She had no experience to draw upon, only instinct—and hers was definitely colored by love.

"Josh around?" she asked as Trent pulled up behind the kitchen.

"He and Mike rode out before your call came. They'll be back later. He does paperwork most evenings after supper, so I guess he'll be up to the house then."

"Don't tell him I'm back," she warned.

Trent stared at her, a grin beginning. "Wouldn't think of it, Becca."

He winked and got out of the truck. Taking her bags up to her room, he grinned again and hastened down the stairs whistling.

Becca unpacked. Taking a quick shower, she donned the stretch jeans and the lacy old-fashioned blouse. She brushed her hair and let it flow freely down her back. Stroking on a touch of mascara and lipstick, she smiled.

It was great to be back in normal clothes. She enjoyed dressing up in New York and dressing down in Key West. But the boots and jeans proved she was home.

Opening her window a crack, she leaned against the sill and gazed out over the range. Tomorrow she'd saddle up and ride. Today it was enough to see the view from her window.

She'd missed it more than she anticipated.

Josh arrived in the late afternoon. She heard him enter the house and walk through to the office. Quietly she gathered her papers and crept down the stairs. She stood in the open doorway for a few minutes feasting her eyes on him as he stood near the desk, leafing through the day's mail that Trent dropped off. He didn't know she was there.

He looked tired, but otherwise great. He tossed his hat on the desk. She noticed instantly he'd had his hair cut. The familiar jeans still delineated his long, muscular legs. His shirt stretched across broad shoulders as he tossed another envelope on a growing stack. She knew he hit a snag when he pushed his fingers through his hair.

"Hi," she said, stepping boldly into the office.

"Becca?"

He turned. For a moment she swore he was stunned,

then pleased. Taking two steps, he swept her up into his arms and swung her around. His mouth lowered to hers and his kiss was long and deep.

Becca clung with delight, savoring the feel of his body against hers, his arms holding her tightly, his mouth bringing her all the happiness she could ever want. Moments, hours, eons later he let her slide down his body until her feet touched the ground. Slowly he raised his head.

"What are you doing here?" he asked, still holding her.

"I live here," she said, pleased with his greeting, even more pleased to notice he hadn't released her.

She felt his buckle against her stomach, his strong fingers tracing her back. The butterflies continued to dance, but had calmed from the cancan to a waltz.

With a greeting like that, maybe, just maybe her gamble would pay off.

She was counting on it.

"I thought you were in Key West," he said, studying her face. "You got a nice tan."

"Almost all over," she said with a grin.

He groaned and leaned his forehead against hers.

"I don't want to hear it," he murmured, his eyes staring deep into hers. "What happened to Key West?"

"I left yesterday."

"That's why I couldn't reach you last night?" he asked.

"Guess so. How are things going here?"

"Worried I can't run the place?"

"No." She hesitated, but it wouldn't get easier, best to plunge ahead. "It's more that I can't stay away."

"I thought you wanted to shake the dust of Wyoming off your feet and never return."

"Sell the ranch, you mean. You thought I'd do that, but I told you I wouldn't."

"How long are you staying?" Slowly he pulled away, his arms falling to his sides.

Taking a step back, he leaned against the edge of the desk, crossing his arms over his chest as he stared at her, the familiar poker face descending.

"Depends," she replied, trying not to feel bereft that he'd let her go.

"On what?"

"On you, actually." She cleared her throat. "I take it you were glad to see me just now."

He nodded.

"I was glad to see you," she said

He waited. The seconds ticked by endlessly. Becca brushed her hands against her jeans in a nervous gesture. She spied her purse on the floor where she'd dropped it when he kissed her. Stooping gracefully, she picked it up and walked to the desk. Placing it on the surface, she was close enough to Josh to feel the radiant heat from his body, to smell his masculine scent.

"Traveling on my own wasn't as much fun as I thought it'd be," she said.

She wanted to reach out and touch him, but couldn't gauge his reaction if she did that.

"I had the best times when I spoke to you at night and told you what I'd done that day."

The phone calls were the highlight of her days.

She'd soaked up the sights and sounds of the various spots she'd visited to share them with him when they talked.

"I liked hearing from you, too," he said slowly. He

reached out and took one of her hands, playing lightly with her fingers. "We missed you here on the Lazy M."

"We?"

"The men."

"Oh."

He laced his fingers through hers and with his other hand tilted up her chin until she gazed deep into his blue eyes.

"I missed you. More than I thought I would. More than I thought possible. Becca—" He hesitated.

She tightened her grip. "What?"

Her heart pounded so hard she could scarcely hear over the sound of the blood rushing through her veins. She didn't want to talk, she wanted to kiss him, to pour all the love she bottled up over him until he hadn't a chance of anything but to love her back.

"I was thinking we make a pretty good team," he said slowly.

"I guess."

A team? Was that all?

"I've got a lot of money saved. Enough that before long I can afford to buy a place."

"Oh, Josh, I don't—"

"Shh. Let me have my say."

His hand cupped her cheek, his fingers brushing into her soft hair, his thumb tracing her lips, swollen and moist from his kiss.

"I was married once before and didn't think I'd ever want to marry again. But I do. I want to marry you. I want you to marry me. It'll be a few years before we can do it, but would you wait for me?"

She held her breath. Had she heard him correctly? He wanted to marry her?

Love exploded and she threw her arms around him.

She'd been right. That one word made a world of difference!

"I love you, Josh Randall. I have for weeks and weeks. I would love to marry you. I don't want to wait, I want to get married right away! I've missed you so much these last weeks."

He hugged her close, burying his face against her neck, his mouth kissing the tender skin, igniting her senses. He trailed kisses to her mouth, plunging in to ravish her until Becca's senses spun.

When they broke apart, both were breathing hard. Becca stretched up against him, encircling his neck with her arms. She wondered if he needed the support of the desk to keep them upright. She needed him to keep her upright.

"It won't be right away. Will you wait?" he asked.

"I don't want to wait."

"Becca, nothing's changed. I'm still just a cowhand. Until I get a place of my own, I don't have anything to offer a wife."

Wife. She smiled.

"I don't care."

"But I do."

She pulled away, cold and scared. The next few minutes could determine whether she got her heart's desire or not.

"Josh, I'm not Tiffany. I'm not going to let you spend the next few years building up the Lazy M and then sell it out from under you."

He nodded.

"You better believe it. It's got to be hard to trust after one experience like that. Especially when our circumstances are similar. But I don't care about your owning a place. If you owned the Lazy M or a ranch in Montana or were a panhandler in New York, I'd still want to marry you and right away. I love you."

It occurred to her with sudden anguish that he hadn't said he loved her. Only that he wanted to marry her. Had Suzanne's insinuations been on target? Did he care for her because she brought the Lazy M with her?

"What about traveling?" he asked.

"We can take some trips together. I didn't enjoy myself alone. When the ranch is prosperous, we'll go places together."

"And college?"

She hesitated. "I'd like to go back to college," she said slowly. "Maybe I can study from here."

"You can go to the university at Laramie."

She nodded. "Come home on weekends."

Her gaze never left his face. She couldn't read his expression. Did he want her to stay? Or go?

Why didn't he tell her he loved her?

Turning away, Becca walked to the window. Gazing out over the hills, she saw nothing. Daring again, she gambled on her own feelings. She felt too strongly about him for Josh to feel nothing in return.

"So we don't get married for a while. I suppose that it would make it all right for me to date while I was in college, then."

Would he recognize the absurdity of the comment? How

could she want to spend an evening with anyone else, loving him as she did?

His long stride carried him across the room in seconds. He spun her around, the poker face gone, blazing anger staring down at her.

"I want you to belong to me, not be out dating other men. But if you can't make do without marriage, then—"

She smiled.

"Wait a minute and let me give you a present I brought for you."

She slipped from beneath his hands and reached for her purse. Taking out the envelope, she handed it to him. Studying his face as he opened it and read the papers, her heart settled in her chest. A warmth like she'd never known filled her.

Josh raised a stunned face. "What in billy blue blazes have you done?"

"Deeded half the Lazy M ranch over to you," she said calmly. "It's yours free and clear. No matter what happens, you have your ranch, Josh. No one can ever take it away from you."

"I can't accept this." He held out the papers. "Even though I know that's what you think this is all about. I remember your accusation that day. I don't want to marry you for a ranch."

"You never denied it. I thought if you had a portion of the ranch, it'd give you whatever security you needed," she explained.

He took a step closer, anger radiating like a bonfire.

"I was so blasted mad at you when you threw that

accusation at me I had to walk away or explode! I don't need your ranch!'"

He thrust the papers at her, his eyes thunderous.

She shrugged and made no move to take them. "It's not my place anymore to tell you what to do with your own property."

"I'll deed it back."

"It's yours to do with what you will."

"Why, Becca? I don't understand." He glanced at the papers again, then looked at her.

"Because, you stubborn cowboy, I wanted to give you something to see if it'd be enough for you to try marriage again. Owning a portion of the ranch will protect you no matter if I sell the other half or not. Besides—" She hesitated and took a deep breath. "I love you more than a ranch. I'm not looking to have you improve it for me so I can sell it. I want someone to share it with me forever."

"I have nothing to bring to you." His fist crumpled the deed.

"I was hoping one day you would love me," she said diffidently.

"Oh honey, I love you to distraction. You must know that!"

He pulled her roughly into his arms, burying his face in her neck, holding on as if for dear life.

She smiled, joy swelling in her heart until she thought it'd burst.

"Then you bring me more than I ever hoped to have. You're thinking of material things. I'm thinking of you yourself. You've taken the burden of the ranch from my shoulders. Being with you promises to be the most exciting thing I'll ever do. You make my heart sing. You'll be my family and you know how much I want a family. I hope together we will have lots of children. But even if we don't, you'll be all I need. I love you, Josh."

"I love you, Becca." He straightened, his hold loosening a bit, enough that he could look into her eyes. "You took a tremendous chance deeding part of the Lazy M to me. What if I didn't love you? What if—"

She shook her head and smiled. "I was banking on you having some feelings. Because of what you said when I left."

He frowned. "What?"

"Don't fall for any other man. I admit I depended heavily on the word other. But I hoped it meant you cared for me. After all the phone calls, all the time we talked on the phone, I knew I loved you more than ever. And I thought maybe you cared."

He swept her up against him and kissed her.

"I more than care, honey. I love you, more than a ranch, more than anything. Marry me and I'll do everything in my power to make you happy."

"Yes. Right away."

"Right away. But I'm still giving you back the land," he murmured against her mouth, scooping her closer for a deep kiss.

She didn't argue. Time enough later to discuss the matter. She only knew now that she'd found her true love. Everything else could be worked out.

It didn't matter who owned the ranch, they'd live on it together. Raise their family together. She had someone to travel with, to share her exploration of new places when they took vacations.

All their dreams would come true.

She had the rest of her life to share with her summer cowboy.

If you liked **Summer Cowboy**,
you'll love the next book in the *Cowboy Hero* series,
Second Chance Cowboy.

If you enjoyed **Summer Cowboy**
please consider leaving a review.

More Books by Barbara McMahon

Cowboy Hero Series
The Cowboy Next Door
Cowboy's Bride
One Stubborn Cowboy
Crazy About a Cowboy
Never Doubt a Cowboy
Cowboy Marshal
Summer Cowboy
Second Chance Cowboy
Movie Star Cowboy

Cowboys of Wildcat Creek
Valentine's Cowboy Rescue
Shelly and the Cowboy
Kristi's Cowboy Hero
Holly's Reluctant Cowboy
A Cowboy for Eliza

Sweet Reunion Romance Collection
Unexpected Reunion
Unpredictable Reunion
Unanticipated Reunion

The Harts of Texas Series
Rebel Heart
Tangled Hearts
Reckless Heart

Sweet Romance Stand-alone Collection
Because of You
Cowboy Charade
I'll Take Forever
Jared's Promise
Mail Order Bride
Not Really Married
Sweet Meant To Be
The Cowboy Comes Home
The Paper Marriage
Trusting Jake
The Banished Bride

www.ingramcontent.com/pod-product-compliance
Lightning Source LLC
Chambersburg PA
CBHW070014260626
47159CB00005B/1797